"I won't give up a marriage that hasn't even begun!"

"And it's not going to!" Vance's authoritative voice brooked no argument. "I'm leaving the hospital this afternoon, Libby. I'll arrange for a taxi to run you to the airport. You can be on the next flight back to London."

"You're not serious," she burst out.

Vance straightened to his full height, his jaw tensed with anger. "I've never been more serious in my life."

"Vance, I'm a twenty-three-year-old woman—not a child you can order around." The words slipped out before she could prevent them.

A dark brow lifted dangerously. "And I'm no longer the man you married. Don't you understand? The accident changed everything. I'm blind, Libby, blind!"

Rebecca Winters, an American writer and mother of four, is a graduate of the University of Utah who has also studied overseas at Swiss and French schools, including the Sorbonne. Currently she is working toward a master's degree in Arabic and teaches French and Spanish in a public school. She is the author of four contemporary romances and several articles, which have appeared in professional magazines. Rebecca's experiences abroad while a student and the friends she met then and in her later travels have all inspired her writing. This is her first book for Harlequin.

Blind
to Love
Rebecca Winters

Harlequin Books

**TORONTO • NEW YORK • LONDON
AMSTERDAM • PARIS • SYDNEY • HAMBURG
STOCKHOLM • ATHENS • TOKYO • MILAN**

ISBN 0-373-02953-5

Harlequin Romance first edition January 1989

CHAPTER ONE

"DR. STILLMAN—are you saying that my husband's blindness is irreversible?" Libby Anson fought for composure. Throughout the long nighttime flight from London to Nairobi, she'd held on to the hope that his condition was temporary, that an operation would restore his sight.

"I'm afraid it is," the doctor answered quietly, extinguishing the little spark of hope that had refused to be quenched until now. He leaned forward in his chair. "When the roof of the mine collapsed, the force caused a tiny fragment of ore to penetrate your husband's skull," he explained. "I'm convinced the nerves in the optic tract were severed, because he can't discern light at all. I'm very sorry."

"I can't believe it." She shook her head, causing the glistening black hair to settle loosely about her shoulders. "Does Vance know his blindness is permanent?"

"Yes. He demanded the truth as soon as he regained consciousness."

"But it's been over two weeks since the accident. I don't understand why someone didn't call me. I'd have come on the next plane. When I think that he's been lying in a hospital bed all this time, and I knew nothing..." Her voice trailed off.

"I assumed he'd been in touch with his family. But the night before last, I learned that he had no visitors or phone calls except from some employees at Anson Mining. So I took the liberty of calling his office to get the phone number of a relative. A Mr. Dean told me that Mr. Anson's next of kin was his father in London, and I phoned him immediately."

Libby frowned. "Hasn't Vance mentioned me at all? I don't understand."

The doctor regarded her fine-boned, oval face, obviously concerned by the troubled expression in her eyes. "Until you appeared on the ward moments ago, I didn't even know Mr. Anson was married. Let alone that he had such a lovely wife," he said in an aside. "Your marriage is a well-kept secret. No one in his company has the slightest idea. How long have you been married?"

Libby sucked in her breath. "Three weeks. Vance had to fly back here right after our wedding ceremony to take care of an emergency at one of the mines. Since he didn't expect to be gone for more than a few days, we decided that I'd stay in London until he could join me, and we could leave on our honeymoon. I've had no word from him since." Her voice trembled as she spoke. "He said he'd be in an inaccessible area of the highlands and that he'd call me as soon as he could." She paused. "Your phone call to his father was the only contact any of us has had." A new wave of pain assailed her. By not acknowledging to anyone that he was married, Vance had wounded her deeply.

"Under the circumstances, you can't know how pleased I am that you're here." The doctor smiled kindly. "I think you've provided me with a missing piece of the puzzle."

Libby uncrossed her long, slender legs and leaned forward. "What puzzle, Dr. Stillman?"

"Your husband is a proud man, but his fierce desire to remain independent in the face of his loss had me worried. Now that I see you, I'm beginning to understand."

"What do you mean?" Libby asked urgently, eyes fastened on his.

He linked both hands behind his head. "If I had a beautiful new bride waiting for me and then suddenly lost my sight, frankly speaking, my first thoughts would probably be suicidal."

"You're not saying Vance doesn't want to live?" she cried out. "Is that why he didn't call me as soon as it happened?"

"Not at all," he hastened to assure her. "But what he *has* done is turn within himself because he can't bear the thought of being dependent—on anyone, but especially on you. He's a brilliant, successful man who's used to being in complete charge. He's built up an enviable mining career here in Kenya. A large corporate staff waits on his decisions. More important, he's acquired a wife and he wants to be all things to her. To *you*. Suddenly his blindness has struck at his very sense of self, his manhood. He's lost faith in his ability to be your protector, breadwinner, lover...."

"Vance is all those things to me, blind or not." Her voice cracked with emotion. "I—I thought you'd phoned Vance's father because you'd been unable to reach me. I didn't know Vance hadn't.... Do most people react like this in his situation? Do they turn away from the people who love them most?"

He averted his eyes and rubbed the pad of his thumb along the edge of the folder in front of him. "A certain amount of depression always accompanies a loss like this, but each case is different, naturally. Like most men, he wants to be the perfect husband, but being blind is an unknown factor—something beyond his control. He's afraid."

Tears filled her eyes. "I can't imagine Vance being afraid of anything."

His brows quirked. "Neither can he...."

Libby blinked as the meaning of his words penetrated her mind. It was always night for Vance now. She couldn't fathom what that would be like. Her heart ached for him, compounding her sorrow. With an effort, she lifted her head. "Is he in pain?"

"Except for an occasional headache, he's in excellent physical shape. I am concerned, however, about the fact that he blames himself for the accident, which took two lives."

Libby gasped softly. She hadn't known, she hadn't thought beyond her husband's own loss.

"I didn't want to discharge him without knowing if he had a close friend or family who'd watch out for him. So far, he's rejected all offers of help. Except for a handful of men from his company, he's refused any visitors. As I explained, I phoned his father to find out what arrangements had been made, if any.

"I have to tell you I'm relieved you've come. Particularly since he insists on leaving the hospital today. He'll put up a fight, but I believe he needs you desperately. Are you up to it?" He eyed her anxiously.

Libby took a deep breath and lifted her chin a fraction. "I need Vance much more than he needs me. I'm his wife and I intend to have a life with him in every sense of the word.''

A smile of relief broke out on the doctor's face. ''Bravo—he's a lucky man to have a woman like you, and I hope that one day soon he realizes it.''

The doctor's words hit upon a growing fear in Libby's heart. Vance had had two weeks to start erecting barriers. The first had been his failure to phone her. ''I'd like to go in and see him now,'' she said decisively, rising to her feet. ''Thank you for your time, Dr. Stillman. I'm grateful you've been here for Vance.''

He stood up and shook her hand. ''Good luck to you, Mrs. Anson. I'll be in to see your husband shortly and answer any questions you may have. Why don't you take him his lunch tray? His appetite isn't quite what it should be, which isn't unusual, of course. But maybe you can succeed where others have failed.''

Libby's fears worsened. ''I'll try.''

''May I ask you a personal question?''

''Of course.'' She stared at him, wondering why he seemed so intent.

''How long have you known your husband?''

''Almost three years. I met him when my step-father bought the stud farm next door to his family's property. Why?''

His eyes narrowed on her profile as she turned to leave. ''I'm relieved to know your marriage wasn't the result of a whirlwind courtship. At least you know what you're up against.''

Libby left his office and shut the door, leaning heavily against it. *Did she really know Vance as well as the doctor assumed?* They might not have had a whirlwind courtship, but with him in Kenya and her away at the International School in Geneva, they'd spent precious little time together. She'd treasured those rare occasions when Vance was able to fly home to see her. When she thought she couldn't bear to say goodbye to him one more time, he'd asked her to marry him, promising her that marriage would solve all their problems.

A shiver rippled over her body as she remembered what Vance had whispered to her at the airport after their wedding. "Now that we have the ceremony out of the way, we can get on with the courtship, Mrs. Anson." His searing kiss with its promise of rapture had been all that sustained Libby for the past few weeks.

She moved away from the door, mentally preparing herself for the first sight of her husband, the conversation that would follow. Somehow she'd find a way to convince him that they would have a wonderful, fulfilling marriage in spite of his blindness. After all, they loved each other. She'd be his eyes! Their physical love would bind them even more closely together. Maybe they'd start a family right away. They both wanted children...unless Vance had changed his mind.

Libby paused beneath the overhead light to examine the rings on her left hand—tangible evidence that their marriage had taken place. A wide band of hammered gold set off the teardrop amethyst. Both the gold and the stone were from the Anson mines, and she remembered how Vance had told her that the color of amethyst always reminded him of her eyes. Suddenly, the desire to be held in his arms had her running down the corridor to the nursing station.

CARRYING VANCE'S LUNCH TRAY, Libby entered the private hospital room.

"You can take that tray back where it came from," Vance's deep voice rang out with all its familiar force. "I'm leaving in a few minutes, and it will only go to waste. Take it to the poor devil next door. He's the one on the bland diet."

After that outburst, Libby hesitated to identify herself. She walked slowly across the room, passing close to him out of necessity.

"I told you I wasn't hungry! For the—" He suddenly broke off talking, and his chin lifted, instantly alert. "That perfume—I thought for a minute..." His voice trailed off and he turned away, running a distracted hand through his dark hair.

Libby's hands shook, causing the teacup to rattle and the covering over the plate to slip. Carefully, she put the tray on the bedside table, then turned to drink her fill of the beloved figure. He was dressed in silk pajamas and a robe, both in a coffee shade. Had a friend or employee brought them from the farmhouse? Were they his taste, or had one of his secretaries purchased them?

Again Libby's confidence was shaken because she hardly knew the Vance who inhabited this part of the world. The bits and pieces of information in his letters and phone calls didn't cover everyday personal habits.

She was stunned by how little his features had changed. The lines around his mouth were deeper, the mold of his lips more cynical, but his masculine beauty was as dominant and devastating as ever. He'd obviously insisted on shaving himself; normally a fastidious person, he'd missed several places. His hair was longer, and he'd lost weight, making him look all of his thirty-one years, but he was still perfect to Libby.

She watched in fascination as he attempted to pack. Items were tossed into the wrong section of the suitcase in haphazard fashion. He swore violently when some of the cassettes slid off the bed and fell to the floor. Cold fingers squeezed Libby's heart as she watched him feel his way around the end of the bed and get down on his hands and knees to search for them.

Without conscious thought, she made a motion to help him find the elusive tapes. Vance's dark head reared back abruptly, like a finely mettled stallion's. Libby gasped involuntarily, unable to help herself. His eyes stared straight ahead, velvety brown and beautiful. But angry! She couldn't believe he wasn't able to see her.

"What in hell do you *want*? You couldn't possibly be Mrs. Grady. She knows better than to try to force me to eat," he remarked in acid tones, making her shudder.

Libby's eyes played over him. No signs of his wound were visible. Dr. Stillman said the tiny shard had entered the skull well past the hairline—an infinitesimal perforation produced by the force of falling debris.

The deep mahogany tan he maintained year-round gave him a deceptively healthy look, though she knew he had to be in a state of shock.

"Have you seen enough, whoever you are?" he snarled at her, making her jump. "Don't you know it's impolite to stare at a blind man?"

Libby was horrified. She didn't recognize the man who inhabited Vance's body. She felt the moisture gather along her brows and chided herself. This would never do. She was reacting in exactly the way she'd sworn she wouldn't.

"Vance?" Her voice trembled with need.

The gasp that finally came out of him sounded like ripping silk. "Dear lord, it *is* you," he whispered, his voice hoarse with shock and with something else as yet undefinable. A whiteness appeared around his taut mouth as he got to his feet. "Libby." It was almost a groan, as if her name had been called forth from some dark, hidden place. But there was an intimate quality in the sound of her name. His voice betrayed intense emotion, and that was something to cherish.

"Yes, Vance." She flew across the hospital room. "You were supposed to come back to London, but under the circumstances, I'll forgive you," she whispered against his lips before locking her arms around his neck and kissing him with an ardor born of all the emotions she'd experienced in the past two days. His body remained rigid, but she hadn't imagined that first brief moment when she'd felt an answering response. Then he was pushing her away and backing around the end of the bed, banging into the handle that raised and lowered it. He cursed again, and his chest heaved as if he were out of breath.

"What are you doing here, Libby?" The cold hostility of his tone alarmed her.

She swallowed hard. "What kind of question is that to ask your wife?"

He thrust his fists into his robe pockets and stood half-turned away from her, his features like stone. "You *know* I don't want you here. I said it all in the letter."

Her heart hammered and she drew closer. "What letter?"

"The letter I dictated to a secretary here at the hospital. She assured me she posted it."

"Vance—I didn't receive your letter. I swear it."

A long silence followed as he assessed the sincerity of her words. "Provided you're telling me the truth, then I don't understand why you're here at all. The plan was that I would get in touch with *you*."

She moistened her lips. "Dr. Stillman called your father yesterday morning and told him about the accident. He phoned me immediately, and as soon as I could make arrangements, I flew out on the next available plane." He paled, and gripped the footboard until his knuckles shone white. "Vance, why didn't you tell me what happened? Why didn't you share something that important? You know I'd have been here in an instant."

She reached over to grasp the hand closest to her. As she pressed his fingers gently, he shook her hand off and backed farther away. She'd never known physical rejection from Vance, and it hurt.

"You shouldn't have come," he muttered grimly. His hand hovered over the things in his suitcase, as if he wanted something to throw. "That letter was sent special delivery. Obviously Dr. Stillman's meddling, however well intended, brought you here before you could receive it. It explained why I don't want you here and why our marriage won't work."

She took a deep breath, trying desperately to remain calm. "Well, now that I'm here, you can tell me in person."

She watched as his other hand felt for the handle of the suitcase. A pulse throbbed at his temples and the whiteness around his lips intensified. "Go home, Libby. There's nothing for you here." He closed the lid but couldn't fasten it because the cord of his shaving kit was in the way.

She'd tried to prepare herself for changes in his behavior, but this harsh cruelty had never been part of him before. He'd turned into a forbidding, implacable stranger. She had an idea that if she made any more physical overtures, he'd push her away bodily. "I am home," she whispered. "We were married three weeks ago and I have the rings to prove it. I believe part of the vows went, 'for better, for worse, in sickness and in health, so long as we both shall live.'"

"I'm blind, Libby. Something far different."

"You're alive!" she flung back on a rush of emotion. "When I heard you'd been in an accident, all I cared about was that you hadn't died. As awful as your blindness must be, it's something we can deal with. I'll help you. I'd do anything for you."

"Wrong, Libby!" She heard him curse beneath his breath. He stood rigidly by the bed, hands clenched. Anyone else would have heeded all the warnings and fled his presence by now. "There's no *we* about it. I told Dr. Stillman. *No visitors.*"

"A wife hardly fits in the same category." She stood her ground. "Why didn't you tell Dr. Stillman you were married? Have you so little faith in me that you thought I might embarrass you in front of your friends and associates here?"

"That's not the reason and you know it." He ran both hands through his dark brown hair in an attitude of abject frustration. "You couldn't possibly understand, Libby."

"Then help me! I love you, Vance. Let me be a wife to you. Please hold me," she begged, starting around the bed toward him.

Vance's eyes narrowed. "Stop it, Libby. The accident changed everything."

"Including your love for me?"

A shadow of pain came and went on his face so quickly that she almost missed it. "I'm not the same man you married. Being blind alters a person's perspective in every conceivable way. It's like being reborn. I have to go my own way. Alone. I'm sorry the letter didn't reach you in time to avoid this unnecessary trip."

"Unnecessary?" A rush of anger swamped her. "You can't alter the fact that we're married, Vance. Since I'm here, the letter is no longer relevant. I refuse to give up on a marriage that hasn't even begun!"

"And it's not going to!" The authoritative tone brooked no argument. "I'm leaving the hospital for the flat this afternoon. I'll arrange for a taxi to run you to the airport. You can be on the next flight back to London."

"You're not serious."

He straightened to his full height, his jaw tensed with anger. "I've never been more serious in my life." His harsh tone convinced her that he meant what he said.

"There are no more flights back to London till morning." She said the first thing that came into her mind, stalling for time. "But if you're that anxious to get rid of me, I'll take a taxi to a hotel."

"No, Libby," came the unexpected comment. "I won't allow you to stay in a hotel alone. You're not familiar with Nairobi. Besides that, you're far too beautiful to be here on your own." He rubbed the back of his bronzed neck in frustration, and mumbled something unintelligible. "I suppose there's nothing for it but to take you back to the flat with me. We can get a taxi to take you to the airport first thing in the morning."

"Vance, I'm a twenty-three-year-old woman—not a child you can order around!" The words slipped out before she could prevent them.

A dark brow lifted dangerously. "And the man you married no longer exists." He stalked to the bathroom and slammed the door.

"Stop feeling sorry for yourself!" she shouted at him angrily.

"Mrs. Anson?"

Libby whirled around, her cheeks hot and the adrenaline pumping through her body. "Dr. Stillman—"

"Why don't you step out into the hall for a minute? I'd like to talk to you."

Libby followed him into the corridor, leaning against the wall for support. The confrontation with Vance had drained her and she felt ill. "You could probably hear us quarreling," she murmured with her head in her hands. "I'm so ashamed for losing my temper like that. But he refuses to let me get close to him, and for a moment, I forgot about his blindness. All I could think of was that he's not going to give us a chance."

"I thought something like this might happen. You have to realize he hasn't accepted his blindness yet. He can't believe he won't see again. That, plus the shock of your being here, is why he's reacting this way."

Libby lifted her head. "But for how much longer? I'm his wife. I love him so much."

He nodded. "I wish I had a pat answer for you, but I don't. You're going to have to give this some time."

"I'm running out of time, doctor. He expects me to fly back to London in the morning."

"The day isn't over yet," he reasoned. "What are your immediate plans?"

Libby blinked to stem the threat of tears. "He says we're going to his flat. Naturally I'd hoped he would want to take me to the farm. When I think of the plans we made..." Her voice faded away.

"Don't give up on your plans. This is only the first day. And please remember that I'm here. You can call me day or night. I've left numbers where I can be reached, along with his discharge papers and pain medication. Keep in mind that the head matron, Mrs. Grady, is experienced in working with the visually handicapped. She can assist you in helping your husband adjust to a daily routine when the time comes. Call her and make an appointment to come in."

Libby smoothed back a strand of hair. She couldn't think past tomorrow morning when Vance intended for her to be on that plane back to England, but she didn't speak her thoughts.

"Thank you again, Dr. Stillman. I've appreciated the talk."

He patted her arm. "Good luck."

Libby stared at his retreating back before slipping into the room once more. While she'd been talking to Dr. Stillman, an orderly had helped Vance change into hip-hugging Levi's and a safari shirt—an outfit he'd often worn when they went riding together. The slight weight loss enhanced his dark, handsome looks, making him appear even taller. Despite the austere expression on his face, he looked wonderful.

"Vance?"

"Where have you been?"

Perhaps she was grasping at straws, but she thought she detected a trace of anxiety mixed with the gruffness of his tone.

"Dr. Stillman wanted to say goodbye and wish us well." His mouth thinned, but he said nothing. "What about your lunch?" she went on. "Aren't you going to eat before we go?"

"What does it take to convince you I'd choke on food right now?"

"Then do you mind if I eat it? I—I haven't had a meal since yesterday afternoon. I know it's silly, but I don't feel well." The light-headedness she'd experienced out in the hall grew worse, and she subsided into one of the chairs near the closet. Waves of nausea washed over her, bathing her in perspiration.

"Libby?"

She didn't imagine the alarm in his voice this time, but she felt too ill to respond.

He felt his way over to her and slid a warm hand beneath her hair to her nape. "Your skin is clammy. Put your head between your legs."

Libby followed his advice, too weak to do anything else. When the buzzing in her ears finally receded, she lifted her head, relishing the feel of his hand against her skin. His fingers worked their way into her hair, massaging her scalp with gentle insistence.

"Better?" With his face this close, she could see the trace of laughter lines around his mouth. She nodded, then realized he couldn't see her. For a moment, she'd forgotten.

"Yes. Much better, thank you."

"Don't move." Her heart filled with love as she watched him try to find his way to the table and search for something for her to eat. After a few mishaps, he managed to come back with a glass of juice.

Libby took it from his hand and drained the contents. The orange juice was lukewarm, but she didn't mind. In a few minutes her strength started to return. "That tasted good."

"Why in the name of heaven didn't you eat on the plane?" he asked, crouching down beside her. His hand found her arm and slid to her wrist, absently feeling for her pulse. The action caused her to tremble.

"Probably for the same reason you didn't eat your lunch." She stifled the urge to draw his dark head to her chest. "I'm all right now, Vance."

She heard him sigh deeply. "You need to eat. I'll call for another tray."

"No. I'll finish yours. Let's not bother anyone." She stood up on still-weak legs and reluctantly pulled out of his grasp. Walking unsteadily over to the table, she began to eat the roll and chicken.

Vance straightened, but with uncharacteristic hesitancy started and stopped several times before reaching the wall phone. He swore as the receiver dropped to the floor, but eventually managed to reach the hospital switchboard and put through a call for a taxi. After that, he made another call. When he didn't speak English, Libby assumed it was Swahili, which he seemed to speak like a native. He replaced the receiver just as the orderly she'd seen earlier appeared in the doorway.

"We're ready for you, Mr. Anson. The wheelchair is directly behind you."

Libby noted the way Vance's hands clenched into fists at his side. "I can walk out of here on my own two legs."

"I know how you feel, sir, but it's hospital policy."

"Vance—" Libby interjected before more arguments could ensue. "Since I came here directly from the airport, I left my luggage down in the reception area. I'll go see about it and meet you at the main doors."

"How much did you bring?"

Her eyes closed. "Everything I own except my horse, King, and Daddy is making arrangements to have him shipped to Mombasa within the week. I thought it would be fun to drive there and pick him up after he's out of quarantine."

His eyes smoldered. He started to say something, but she slipped out of the room beyond earshot. All the way to the foyer, she kept recalling her stepfather's words. "Vance has been blessed with a greater gift than his eyesight, and that's your love, honey." It was easy enough for her stepfather to say. After the death of Libby's natural father, her mother had married a widower who'd never had children of his own. Libby filled the void in his life and he doted on her. They'd been a happy family, open in their affection. But Libby knew it would take a lot more than love to help Vance now.

CHAPTER TWO

"IS YOUR NAME ANSON?" The man addressing Libby climbed out of a taxi.

"Yes. My husband will be ready any minute."

The man scratched his head as he surveyed the amount of luggage surrounding her. "Is this everything?"

"No. My husband has a suitcase."

The driver muttered something in his native tongue and started loading bags into the rack on top of the vintage Peugeot. What he couldn't fit there he piled next to the driver's seat. "You get in back and I'll put one of the cases at your feet."

Libby did as he suggested, realizing it would be a tight squeeze. Moments later, she caught sight of Vance being wheeled out the front doors of the hospital. The afternoon sun glinted in his hair, highlighting the chestnut tones blended with the brown. In sunglasses, he looked perfectly normal, but she could sense from his taut features the kind of tension that gripped him. It took a rare sort of courage to leave the hospital and the security it offered. Libby recognized this was a moment Vance had to struggle through alone, but she still felt excluded.

The consequences of his loss were beginning to make their impact. She felt angry all over again that his blindness had the power to rob their relationship of its former intimacy. The closeness, the sharing—that all seemed to have fled. He lived in his own world now, and she didn't have the faintest idea how it felt, or how to gain entrance.

"Here's your cane, Mr. Anson. Compliments of the hospital floor!" The orderly put it on Vance's lap, but he immediately pushed it away.

"I have no use for this. If I have to resort to a cane, I might as well walk around with a microphone telling everyone I'm blind."

Libby was aghast at Vance's rudeness, but the orderly appeared unperturbed as he steadied the wheelchair. Vance put a hand on the frame of the open door and started to climb in back. Inadvertently, his other hand brushed against the curve of her hip. She felt its heat through the thin fabric of her cotton shirtwaist. Her body quickened when his hand trailed to her thigh; it was as if he needed to touch her and couldn't help himself. The intimacy of the moment forced a soft gasp from her that he must have heard. He immediately withdrew his hand and sat back as the door closed, careful not to have any contact with her in spite of his long legs.

Libby couldn't take her eyes off him. His dark good looks filled her vision to the exclusion of anything else and increased her longing to hold him close. Her body was still reacting to the touch of his hand and her heart thrilled at the undeniable proof that he desired her, however much he might want her out of his blind world.

The driver started the engine and drove out into the stream of traffic. He maneuvered the battered taxi with death-defying skill through the crowds of honking cars and noisy people. She listened to the volatile exchanges coming through the open window. "Vance," she ventured, stretching her hand to his bronzed forearm without thinking. He flinched as if the warm touch of her fingers scalded him. She quickly removed them. "Everyone sounds angry."

Vance sat rigidly staring straight ahead. "Swahili is an animated language. The natives shout it quite naturally. You get used to it," he muttered, sounding far away from her just then. He remained silent throughout the rest of their journey to his flat.

The driver drove like a maniac, but so did everyone else. It was another thing she'd have to get used to. Because, despite Vance's edict that she return to London, she had no intention of leaving him.

In a few minutes, the taxi came to a stop in front of a modern, five-story apartment building in the heart of the city. Vance had once explained that his corporate office was within walking distance of the flat for easy access. In a way, she was thankful for the flat; it would allow her, finally, to be alone with him—away from everyone else. Maybe then she could try to reason with him, secure in the knowledge that no one would interrupt them.

"The driver will take the bags to the lobby, and the concierge will let you inside the flat," Vance explained, causing her spirits to plummet to a new low.

"Where are you going?" She tried to sound interested rather than devastated by the unexpected arrangements. Everything in her wanted to cry out at this injustice that prevented him from loving her. Until the accident, Vance could hardly bear to have her out of his arms for any reason. Now he couldn't wait to be rid of her.

"I have things to do at the office, Libby, and I have no idea what time I'll get back tonight so don't wait up for me. I've asked the concierge to put groceries in the kitchen, so you'll be able to eat when you want. Don't go outside if you get restless. You can watch TV if you're bored, but under no circumstances do I want you wandering around downtown Nairobi unescorted. Do you understand?"

He'd always been protective of her, but right now his concern seemed obsessive. Still, she had no desire to add to his anxieties. "I'm going to bed. Jet lag has caught up with me. I did promise to phone the parents and let them know I'd arrived safely. Do you mind if I call your father and tell him you're all right? Naturally, he's worried."

He gave an exasperated sigh. "I don't see the necessity since you'll be back home tomorrow night. But I suppose it would be a good idea to let them know so they can make arrangements to meet your plane."

That hateful, patronizing arrogance aroused her anger again. She whirled around and reached for her train case. The driver transported the rest of her luggage to the door of the apartment building. Another man who appeared on the porch indicated he was the concierge and that Libby should follow him.

She glanced over her shoulder, anxious for Vance in spite of her churning emotions. She had to suppress the urge to warn him to be careful, to remind him that it was his first day out of the hospital. His stern profile daunted her. This was the side of him presented to the business and professional world. A man in command—strong, shrewd. Without such leadership qualities he could never have carved out an empire for himself in this still-primitive land. But Libby knew a tender, softer side of Vance. An ache passed through her body as she wondered if she would ever see that side of him again.

She shielded her eyes from the blazing sun. "I'll give Winslow your love. See you later," she called after him. But Vance made no acknowledgment. The driver returned to the taxi and they sped off into the afternoon traffic.

A searing pain racked her body as her eyes followed the path of the taxi until it was out of sight. Afraid she'd break down in front of the concierge, she hurriedly followed him into the building and accompanied him to the third floor. "The building has security, Mrs. Anson. No one can come in through the door without a special key. You'll be safe here."

Libby whispered a quick thank-you and closed the door, falling against it as deep, choking sobs welled up inside her. Huddled there, next to the door, she gave way to her despair. Pressing her knuckles to her mouth, Libby sobbed out the anger at the unfairness of it all, her grief at Vance's resistance to her overtures of love. Mingled with her sorrow over his blindness was this devastating ache she couldn't assuage. The loss of his sight seemed to have robbed him of the ability to reach out to anyone. Particularly his wife.

Unaware of the passage of time, Libby relived those first moments in the hospital room when she'd thrown her arms around him and kissed him. Caught off guard, he'd responded with all the old hunger and passion—until he remembered his blindness. Then he'd pulled away and retreated behind his barriers. It occurred to Libby that the Vance she'd fallen in love with was still there, buried beneath layers of pain and bitterness. But how to find that man again? She *had* to if she ever hoped to experience happiness again. Raging against the fates that had brought them to this point would accomplish nothing.

On a sniff of determination, Libby wiped her eyes and moved away from the door, suddenly aware of her surroundings. She made a cursory inspection. The serviceable, two bedroom flat, which came furnished in pseudo-Mediterranean decor, was obviously not a place that reflected Vance's personality but one that simply met his needs when he worked in Nairobi.

Kicking off her sandals, she padded into the kitchen and warmed a tin of soup so she wouldn't feel faint again. But halfway through the meal she lost her appetite completely and headed for the bathroom to take a shower. A while later, after making the phone calls to reassure the families, she prepared for bed.

Though her French lace nightgown would be wasted on Vance, she had a need to pretend she was a bride as she slipped beneath the covers. He'd shattered her dreams of what their honeymoon was going to be like. Libby couldn't forget that she should have been lying in his arms right then, loving him and being loved. His determination to send her out of his life tormented her, but her body begged for sleep.

She finally succumbed, burrowing her face in the pillow where the faint trace of Vance's cologne still lingered. Hot tears trickled out of the corners of her eyes as she fell into a troubled sleep.

The flat was pitch-black when she awoke hours later. A noise disturbed her and she sat up in bed with a start. Had Vance come home?

Her ears strained to listen as she heard him bumping into something and swearing softly under his breath. He hadn't yet had a chance to feel his way around the flat. She threw off the covers and slid out of bed, hurrying into the hall to turn on a light.

Out of the corner of her eye, she caught a glimpse of movement. Vance had just settled down for the night in the guest bedroom. His dark tousled head moved restlessly on the pillow as he attempted to get into a comfortable position. His bronzed shoulders were visible above the covers.

Libby's heart melted with love for him. Full of resolve, she moved over to the bed and put a hand on his leg. "Vance?"

He jackknifed into a sitting position, taking part of the covers with him. "What do you think you're doing?"

Libby recoiled instantly. His furious outburst reopened the wound inflicted earlier. "I came to tell you you got into the wrong bed." She moistened her dry lips. "You promised me that when we were together again, we'd go someplace private, and you'd never let me out of your arms. I've been living for that, Vance. I've ached for you...."

In a lightning move, he flung himself from the bed, and shrugged into the same brown robe he'd worn at the hospital. "Since you're awake, we might as well have a talk, Libby. Come into the other room."

No matter how hard she tried to brace herself against his continual rejection of her, she couldn't get used to the searing pain that accompanied it. As she followed him into the living room, she had to force herself to keep from helping him. He bumped into several pieces of furniture before he reached his destination. He looked haggard—tortured even—and raked a suntanned hand through his dark hair. Libby caught glints of the rich mahogany color as he disheveled it with his fingers.

Concern for his well-being took precedence over her own pain. "Are you hungry, Vance?"

His chest rose and fell. "Food's the last thing on my mind."

"I'm sure it's been a horrendous day, but you still need something to eat," she said softly. "I'll make supper." Not waiting for a response, she hurried through the dining area to the kitchen. In a matter of minutes, she had water boiling and sandwiches made.

"I told you. I'm not hungry." She hadn't heard him come to the doorway.

"Perhaps not, but I am." She put a plate of ham and tomato sandwiches on the table, then followed with the instant coffee, which she preferred to tea. Vance was still standing at the kitchen entrance as she sat down and took a bite of sandwich. She fastened her attention on him. Despite his dark tan, he looked like a man who bore the weight of the world on his shoulders. Dr. Stillman's observation about Vance's depressed state worried her, as well. "Won't you at least sit down while I eat? You look exhausted."

He rubbed the back of his neck, something she'd occasionally seen him do when he felt frustrated or preoccupied. "Did anyone call the flat while I was out?"

"Not that I'm aware of. I fell asleep shortly after the concierge let me in. Were you expecting an important call?"

He dismissed her question with a vague gesture, putting his hands in his robe pockets. "Have you had any recurrence of the nausea you experienced this morning?"

In the face of everything, his protective instincts still prevailed, making her love him all the more. "No. None. I'm convinced it was simply low blood sugar and no sleep. The person I'm worried about is you." She couldn't keep her concerns bottled up any longer. "You're barely out of the hospital. I'm sure Dr. Still-man would agree with me that—"

"Don't say another word!" he cut in on her almost brutally. "You sound suspiciously like a wife, and I have enough to deal with already." His face dark-ened. "How can I make you understand that I'm not the same man you knew in England? You seem to be treating this as a temporary setback. I assure you it isn't."

Her chin went up. "I can remember telling you the same thing a couple of years ago, when you forced me to get back on King after I fell off. I broke two ribs and felt like death, but once my injuries had healed, *you* made me go down to the stable and climb back in the saddle. When everyone else was ready to coddle me, you ignored my misgivings and persisted until I found the courage to face my fear. I was so terrified, I didn't think I'd ever be able to get close to King again, but the Vance I knew wouldn't let me give up!"

His face closed as he advanced slowly into the kitchen, feeling for the nearest chair. "I'm blind, Libby. Blind!" he said with such emotion the cords stood out in his neck. "You could have no possible conception of what that means. We're not talking about a few broken bones. I'll never be able to read another blueprint . . . survey a site—let alone drive to one—never take another step without a damn cane to keep me from crashing into walls. How does it feel to know your husband can't see to protect one hair on your head?''

In a fierce, sweeping gesture to drive home his point, his hand accidentally knocked over the coffee mug nearest him and it pitched to the floor. Libby jumped up from the table in surprise and dashed to the sink for a cloth.

"Dear lord—did I burn you?" He felt his way over to the sink, his hand brushing against her forearm.

"No. It's nothing," Libby hastened to reassure him, hearing the torment in his voice. "The coffee wasn't that hot." She felt a curious languor as his hands ran up and down her bare arms. They stood so close, the scent of her perfume and the male tang of his skin combined to form a heady stimulant. His breath on her lips sent a voluptuous warmth through her body. "Only a few drops spilled on my nightgown." Unable to do otherwise, she melted against him.

For a split second, his dark face descended and she lifted her mouth expectantly for his kiss, aching for him with every heartbeat. Then she heard his sharp intake of breath before he pushed her away from him.

A moan sounded low in her throat as he wheeled around and felt for the nearest chair back. The unexpected moment of closeness and intimacy had passed, leaving her totally bereft. He stood rigidly by the chair while she cleaned up the liquid on the floor. Fortunately the mug hadn't shattered.

"I'm not only helpless, I'm dangerous." The self-loathing in his voice shocked her.

"Don't talk like that, Vance." She gave in to the impulse to press herself against his back, sliding her hands up his arms. But he moved away abruptly with none of his earlier gentleness, forcing her arms to fall to her sides. "You've always made me feel safe. Your blindness has nothing to do with it. You must know that."

He swore violently as he turned around in her direction. His handsome features were distorted by lines of rage. "I can't even find you!"

"The accident barely happened. Give it more time. Give us more time," she begged.

"Time?" A harsh laugh ripped out of him. "You don't seem to understand, Libby. My blindness isn't going to get better. Your husband isn't whole. When are you going to face that fact?"

"You're feeling sorry for yourself again." It killed her to say it when her instincts told her to wrap her arms around him and absorb his pain. His head reared back in fury, but she forced herself to go on. "All right, you've lost your sight, and I can't imagine how it must feel, but you seem to have lost your nerve as well as your charm along with it."

A dark, ruddy color stained his cheeks. "Who taught you how to hit a man below the belt? I would never have suspected it of you."

Libby hugged her arms to her chest, shaking at her own temerity. "There's a lot you don't know about me. Unfortunately, this accident has revealed something about you that I never knew before. I just hope you don't treat your employees like you're treating me. You have an enviable reputation, according to Dr. Stillman. He told me how successful and brilliant you are—a man in charge of your own destiny. It might be to your advantage if everyone goes on believing that! Don't worry, I won't let on to anyone that you're giving up so soon."

"That's right, because you won't be here!" he rasped, slamming his fist on the table so hard the sandwich plate jumped.

Libby shrank from his anger. "I can see there's no getting through to you right now. I'd hoped we'd be able to work things out, but it seems I was wrong."

"Libby!" he shouted as she fled past him and ran to the bedroom, slamming the door. He wasn't far behind. Before she could catch her breath, the door flew open. "Don't ever run out on me like that again." His voice contained a veiled threat. "I'm not through with you."

She spun around on her heels. "I thought you were. What I don't understand is why you married me in the first place. We took vows before God. Didn't they mean anything to you?"

"There was no altar, Libby."

In shocked silence, she took a step toward him. The blood drained from her face. "You mean, because we weren't married in a church you don't consider the ceremony binding? How dare you say that?" A blackness swept over her. "Here." She pulled off her wedding rings and dropped them in his robe pocket. With their bodies almost touching, she could detect the sudden pallor of his face.

"Stay here alone, my beloved husband. Wallow in your dark world and enjoy your misery. Don't ever take risks. Don't ever let anybody get close to you. Least of all your *wife*." She closed the door in his face, already regretting her impulsive actions.

Those rings had been part of her. The night he'd flown to Switzerland to surprise her with the engagement ring was the most thrilling night of her life. Until then, she hadn't known the depth of his love; now, she'd thrown the rings back at him. It hadn't even been twelve hours since they left the hospital. Vance was still just as intent on forcing her to give up, and once again, she'd let him get to her. *Would she never learn?*

Throughout the rest of the night, Libby went over their bitter exchange in her mind. They'd both said things that were calculated to injure beyond the ability to heal. Like water bursting over a dam, words had tumbled out of her mouth—words she couldn't take back. In the heat of the moment, she'd forgotten his suffering because she'd been so overwhelmed by her own needs.

His tortured attempt to explain what blindness was like began to make inroads on her mind. Guilt consumed her as she absorbed the full impact of what he'd been trying to tell her—to impress upon her. How had she dared say those things to him? If their positions were reversed, wouldn't she have done everything in her power to break off with Vance? To free him from a bondage not of his own choosing? And yet...*wouldn't she have wanted him to fight for her anyway? Wouldn't she be devastated if he gave up so easily?*

Not having closed her eyes all night, Libby was grateful for morning. She felt an overpowering need to talk to Vance one more time. If they could start over again... If there could be a new beginning...

She'd never been prone to headaches, but when she got out of bed, the pain at the back of her skull made her slightly ill. Her eyes burned. Had Vance lain awake all night, too—waiting for morning to come so he could send her back to England? She hadn't heard a sound since awakening.

After making the bed, she dressed in aqua-colored cotton pants and top, securing her hair with a chiffon scarf in a lighter shade of the same hue. A minimum of makeup and she was ready to go in search of her husband. In spite of everything that had happened, in spite of everything that had been said, she was determined to make their marriage work.

The moment she stepped into the hallway she heard voices coming from the living room. They were too low for her to distinguish individual words, but their visitor was male.

Like an incoming tide, rage churned inside her again. Vance had done this to prevent a scene. He'd taken every precaution to ensure that she didn't miss her plane, cutting off their last hope of communication. *What could she do? Pretend to be too ill to leave the flat?* Vance would never believe her. He was prepared for every conceivable argument. The only thing to do was let him have his way. She'd go to the airport. But it didn't mean she'd get on the plane. What Vance didn't understand was that for her, a life without him couldn't be any worse than being blind.

"Mrs. Anson." A man with a build like a rugby player and a shock of white-blond hair stood up as Libby entered the room. She estimated him to be in his late forties. His glance was sharply appraising, which didn't surprise her since Vance had told no one of her existence. "I'm Martin Dean, filling in until the boss is back in the office. It's a pleasure." He extended his callused hand in greeting.

"How do you do." Libby shook his hand, looking from him to her husband. Her pulse quickened as she gazed at Vance. He stood in the middle of the room with his strong legs astride, dressed in blue jeans and

a dark green pullover. He looked relaxed and at ease,
and certainly nothing like the implacable man he'd
been last night.

"I'm so sorry about barging in on your honeymoon. Vance is a deep one. May I congratulate you on
your marriage? I had no idea until moments ago that
Vance had a wife to come home to." His glance flicked
to the taller man. It gave Libby a chance to study
Vance's second in command. Trusted enough to be put
in charge during Vance's absence, he'd nevertheless
been kept in the dark about their marriage. "Your
taste is impeccable, old chap." He grinned at her as he
spoke. "No wonder you kept flying to Switzerland."

"Well, she's here now, thank God," Vance murmured with such emotion Libby was stunned.
"Sweetheart?" He held out a beckoning hand. Libby
couldn't believe this was happening, but she needed no
prodding to lessen the distance that separated them.
His hand closed possessively over hers as soon as she
reached him. "Did we waken you?" he whispered,
brushing his mouth against her cheek the way he used
to.

Libby could hardly breathe. "No. In fact, the flat
seemed so quiet, I thought you'd gone out."

His arm went around her slender shoulders and he
pulled her close. "Not a chance, Mrs. Anson." Then
he lowered his mouth to hers in a hard, lingering kiss.
The contact made Libby reel. Caught off guard, she
swayed and felt his other arm go around her for support.

Martin started to chuckle. "Maybe I'd better wait
outside in the Land Rover. Or better yet, why don't I
go to work and pick you two up this afternoon? I
shouldn't have intruded."

Vance took his time about lifting his head. "Don't apologize, Martin. You had no way of knowing I was keeping Libby to myself. Fortunately, my beautiful wife and I will have all the time alone we want when we get to the farm." Her astonished gasp was stifled once more by the pressure of his mouth as he sought a more satisfying response from her. For some unknown reason, Vance wanted the other man to witness this display of husbandly affection. He demanded her cooperation with the matchless mastery of the old Vance.

He drank deeply, pulling her into a whirlpool of desire. She forgot everything. The pain, the cruelty, the rejection. Obviously reluctant, he let her go. "Maybe you'd better grab a bite to eat before we embarrass Martin further," he whispered after lifting his head. "He's offered to drive us to the farm. If your case is packed, he'll take it out to the car."

Without his arm around her shoulder, Libby would have fallen. She averted her eyes from Martin's interested gaze. "I'll hurry." She headed for the kitchen in a weakened state, full of unanswered questions. But whatever Vance's motives, he didn't plan to send her away after all.

She made toast and poured milk, but her thoughts centered on her husband's sudden about-face. Her fingers went to her lips, which still tingled from the pressure of his kiss. Had he, too, regretted their words of last night? Did he waken wanting to start all over again? She hadn't imagined the hunger in his kiss. At some point, he'd forgotten the other man's presence, just as she had. Surely this meant that Vance wanted to make their marriage a real one, that he'd realized how cruel, how unnecessary, it would be to go on denying them what they both craved. The farmhouse represented home and a fresh start.

When Libby finished eating and she'd tidied the kitchen, all the bags had been taken out of the flat. Martin assisted Vance to the Land Rover. This time, Vance climbed into the back seat ahead of Libby. When it was her turn, he grasped her wrist and pulled her onto the seat beside him, pressing a kiss to the side of her neck.

"You can put the rest of her things in front with you, Martin," he called out the open window. "I intend to enjoy my wife's company during the drive."

"I understand completely." His man-to-man laugh floated through the open window as he arranged the luggage to his satisfaction. Occasionally, Libby caught him glancing inside at the two of them. Their marriage had clearly come as a shock to him. Perhaps he felt slighted because Vance had chosen to keep it a secret. After all, the two men worked closely together.

While Martin was busy, Vance took advantage of their brief privacy. He reached for Libby's hand and held it fast. But his tone was reserved, even formal. "The discussion I wanted to have with you last night got out of hand. There are things we need to talk over in a rational manner—as you so succinctly pointed out to me—so we're going to the farm where the atmosphere is more conducive to the kind of conversation I have in mind. I'd appreciate it if you'd hold your questions until we're alone. I prefer to keep our private life private." He whispered the last as Martin opened the door and swung his compact body into the driver's seat to start the motor.

Vance's words dashed her hopes once more. His amorous performance had been solely for Martin's benefit. An ache passed through her body as Vance lifted her hand to his mouth and kissed the palm—a calculated cruelty under the circumstances.

Unwilling to suffer through this alone, Libby nestled closer to Vance and brushed her mouth against his. "How far is the farm?"

His chest rose and fell noticeably. "An hour from Nairobi."

"How lovely." She spoke the words at the corner of his taut mouth and had the satisfaction of feeling his body tense.

"Martin . . . as long as you've offered your services, will you drive us by the Bantu pharmacopoeia on our way out of the city? Libby shouldn't miss it."

Vance had once written her about the native bazaar, which sold everything from monkey skulls to fried porcupine. She derived immense pleasure from the fact that her nearness forced him to rely on counteractive measures to combat it.

She settled against him, her hand still in his. If nothing else, a sight-seeing jaunt would give her more time like this, sitting quietly close to Vance. More time to feel like the hopeful young bride she was pretending to be.

CHAPTER THREE

THE MAU ESCARPMENT rose nine thousand feet. The farm was located near the six-thousand-foot level where the air was thinner. A few tufts of white cloud passed overhead, but it was a beautiful June morning, warm and fresh.

As the Land Rover drew closer to its destination, Libby noticed the absence of villages. In their place were patches of evergreen forest separated by wide expanses of grassland. An occasional native tending a flock of impala would wave to them as they drove farther into the highlands.

Libby lifted her head from Vance's broad shoulder and studied his aquiline features. He'd fallen asleep, head resting against the back of the seat. The dark shadows beneath his eyes led her to believe he'd tossed and turned all night, as she had. He looked vulnerable, with his compelling mouth softened in repose, and with tendrils of dark brown hair spilling over his tanned forehead.

She relished the feel of his ripcord-strong leg brushing against hers. Her glance rested on their hands entwined on his hard thigh. In sleep, Vance hadn't let go of her. All the bitterness of the night before seemed to have faded away, but she knew this respite was only temporary.

Vance awakened when Martin drove the Land Rover around a sharp corner and geared down to a dirt road. Tightening her grip on his hand, Libby gazed out her window. Cultivated fields with row after row of blossoming fruit trees greeted her vision. In the far distance she noticed a copse of oak trees. The car drew closer and she saw a snowy-white Dutch farmhouse glittering in the sunlight. The oaks formed lacelike shadows against the exterior.

The house reminded her of the charming Hampshire barns she'd seen in England. Vance explained that a transplanted Dutchman had come to Kenya in the late 1800s, and had incorporated the local one-story farmhouse with the Amsterdam gable—the important gable placed over the front door to contain the attic. The effect was exquisite. Farther on she could see a group of outbuildings surrounded by wildflowers of every hue and description.

"How incredibly beautiful it is," she cried as Martin stopped the Land Rover. Vance relinquished his hold on her, and Libby climbed out of the seat to survey her kingdom. She sucked in her breath. "Oh, Vance...I had no idea." She gazed heavenward. At this elevation, the sky was an intense blue, and the temperature that of a delightful spring day. There would be plenty of light for a herb garden.

Her gaze was drawn to the window facing west with its leaded panes. Frothy lace curtains peeked through. Vance had accomplished more than she'd realized since they made their wedding plans. A fresh wave of love and longing swept over her. Her eyes sought her husband, but he was busy helping Martin with their bags.

Libby remained motionless, worshiping this tall, darkly tanned man who had such inherent authority and power, yet could display infinite tenderness. Her eyes played over him, admiring the fit of his clothes, the lean tautness of his muscles.

"I can't wait to see inside, Vance," she called out and started to pick up some of the supplies stowed in the back of the car. Though she wanted to put her arm through his, she didn't dare. His efforts to do as much as possible without Martin's assistance pleased her. She didn't want to interfere or impede his progress, particularly in front of the other man. If her eyes didn't deceive her, he seemed to move with a determination that had been missing yesterday. Perhaps he'd put on this air of confidence for Martin's benefit, but the results were gratifying. Surely Vance could see that he functioned beautifully when he gave himself half a chance.

"Libby?" Vance paused on the porch while Martin went inside the house with more luggage. "Will you forgive me if I talk to Martin before he goes back to Nairobi? I promise it won't take long."

She walked up to him and pressed another kiss to his firm chin. "Don't worry about me. I'm dying to explore the house."

Vance stood there with his hands on his hips, an expression of barely controlled patience on his face. Martin reappeared in the doorway, then, but fortunately, Vance was facing Libby.

She smiled at the other man. "Thank you for driving us out here, Mr. Dean. You can't possibly know how excited I am to be home. And now I'll leave the two of you alone so you can talk business." She raised up on tiptoe and kissed her husband lightly on the lips, aware of the other man's scrutiny.

"Please call me Martin, Mrs. Anson. We don't stand on ceremony here. My wife and I will be extending an invitation to dinner one day soon. That is, when Vance here is willing to share you. Or should I say if?" he amended with a grin.

Libby's gaze flicked back to her husband. "We'll look forward to it, won't we, Vance?"

"Marj is an excellent cook." It was an answer of sorts. Libby squeezed Vance's hand and proceeded into the farmhouse.

Her first impression was one of airiness and light—white walls with splashes of vivid color from native African fabrics and dark-toned woods indigenous to the area—exactly as she and Vance had planned. The reality far surpassed her wildest expectations.

The central hallway was flanked on one side by a living room and library. To the right was the dining room and beyond it, the kitchen. The bedrooms were located at the rear.

Libby mused that Vance must have moved heaven and earth to have the walls treated and ready for paint this fast. The only rooms ready for occupancy were their bedroom, the kitchen, bathroom and library. Everything else required paint, floor coverings and window treatment—projects she and Vance could carry out together. She experienced a great thrill as she imagined the finished interior with colorful native area rugs and furniture, interspersed with treasured family heirlooms. Her eyes grew misty. How she'd longed for this moment . . .

Excitement gripped her as she carried her train case to the master bedroom—the room with the Swiss lace curtains showing through the window. From a brief comment she'd once made about that particular fabric, he'd created a room of great beauty. It meant that he'd planned to marry her long before they'd even become officially engaged; something she hadn't really known before this moment. This knowledge took her breath away. She sank down on the double bed and gazed about her, taking in the armoire, built-in dresser and fabulous area rug of African origin. Vance had chosen an apple-green motif with native accents. She couldn't fault his taste.

A photograph propped on the dresser drew her attention. Vance must have had it enlarged from pictures he'd taken when he visited her in Lausanne. She stood beneath a Gothic arch at the Château de Chillon with the battlements in the background. She'd worn her black hair even longer then. The fact that he'd gone to the trouble of preserving this particular picture touched her deeply. He'd proposed to her on that trip. Libby had a dozen favorite photographs of Vance she intended to add to the dresser. She refused to entertain any ideas of leaving Kenya, and certainly not on this glorious day.

On her way to the kitchen, she peeked inside the other two bedrooms. The one on the north would make a perfect nursery. She dreamed about having Vance's baby, perhaps in a year or two. Already, her mind was filled with ideas for decorating the empty room.

The other bedroom came as something of a surprise because the walls needed to be repaired. There was evidence of a fire, though she couldn't tell how recent. Vance had purchased the farm when he first came to Kenya, but he hadn't started major renovations until he asked Libby to marry him, and it had stood vacant for several years.

She knew the kitchen was her favorite room in the farmhouse as soon as she entered it. A huge, ceramic-glazed fireplace with authentic blue Delft tiles dominated one wall. It dated back to the building's origins, and the scene was as quaint as the old quarter of Amsterdam. She understood why Vance had been charmed by its beauty. From the previous owner, he'd inherited an antique oak table—rectangular in shape—with four intricately hand-carved chairs. Obviously he intended to keep and restore as much of the original farmhouse as possible. The whole idea enchanted Libby.

Sitting at the table, she could look out the mullioned windows to a glorious vista of blossoming fruit trees that stretched as far as the eye could see. The delightful view captured her attention for a long time. Vance had found paradise here. Resolving to share it with him, she took a deep breath and looked about her to see what should be done first. Martin had brought in the boxes containing food stores. She'd be able to acquaint herself with the kitchen's layout as she put things away.

A double sink and new plumbing had been installed. The old oak floors had been sanded and stained to a gleaming amber color. She reflected that in everything he did, Vance was a perfectionist. He'd created an efficient, fully functional room, yet he'd retained all the warmth and charm intended by the first owner. What an irony that anyone so artistic, so aware of beauty, should have his sight taken away...

By the time Libby had emptied the boxes it was noon, and she found that she was hungry. Hoping

Vance's appetite had returned, she proceeded to fix lunch, then walked through the house to the library in search of both men. Martin would probably need a meal before he returned to Nairobi, she thought. But when she reached the front hall, she heard the sound of the Land Rover. Vance was in the act of shutting the door.

"Vance, I was just coming to tell both of you that lunch was ready."

He stiffened at the sound of her voice. "He had to get back in a hurry. We're alone, Libby."

Something in his tone sent an apprehensive chill down her spine. Gone was the attentive lover of the morning.

"I'm afraid our lunch isn't terribly interesting. Soup and sandwiches. But I promise to do justice to our evening meal." When he didn't respond, she turned and walked back toward the kitchen. He followed with some difficulty, feeling the walls until he entered the kitchen and found a chair. To her surprise he sat down and began touching everything carefully. She moved a plate of food in front of him. "I used the ham from last night, but maybe it doesn't appeal."

"I couldn't care less what I eat. However, I happen to know you're an excellent cook, so stop hovering." Libby swallowed a retort as she saw him actually pick up a sandwich and begin to eat. Not only that, but he seemed to enjoy it and ate with apparent appetite. She'd begun to wonder how long he could go without sustenance. He ate everything on his plate and drained his glass of milk with few accidents.

"Did you and Martin get some work done?" she asked conversationally. Vance was being too quiet, and she feared that his silence portended more depression. Right now she didn't want anything to mar the magic of their first meal together in their new house. For a little while she wanted to pretend that everything was normal.

"Unfortunately not. He found your presence to be a more interesting topic."

Libby took a deep breath. "Why didn't you tell him about our marriage? It put him in an awkward position."

He lay down his fork. "If you recall, the wedding was so quickly planned, it would have been difficult to let anyone know. Besides, I'd intended to introduce you to my staff at a formal reception, here at the farm. But I don't want to discuss that right now."

Libby eyed her husband, unable to gauge his mood. "The farmhouse—the orchards—everything is so beautiful, I can't believe it, Vance."

His features hardened perceptibly. "Save it, Libby. Now that we have all the preliminaries out of the way, I want to talk to you, but I want your promise that you won't interrupt until I'm finished."

She blinked. "You have it."

"I hope you mean that," he said in a sober voice, "because when you hear what I have to say, you're not going to like it." His words struck a chord of fear in Libby's heart. "When you appeared in my hospital room yesterday—unannounced *and* uninvited, I might add—I could have strangled you with my bare hands."

The venom in his tone made Libby quail. She looked down at her empty plate. How could he change from loving husband so quickly?

"I believe you when you tell me you didn't get my letter. Knowing you as I do, you wouldn't have left a stone unturned to talk to me on the phone, if it *had* arrived. Unfortunately, if you'd waited in London another twelve hours after hearing about the accident, you would have received it. In your haste to fly to my side," he began in that hateful, mocking tone, "you made your presence known to everyone in sight. By playing your wifely role to the hilt in front of Dr. Stillman, you've caused a series of consequences that have put you, me and my company in more jeopardy."

"What?" she gasped aloud, lifting her head.

His beautiful mouth curved into a cruel line. "You promised."

At this point, Libby started to shake and couldn't stop.

Vance pushed himself away from the table and stretched his long legs to the side, his arms folded across his chest. "I have an enemy, Libby. Someone within my company is out to ruin me, and maybe they've succeeded. The mine collapse was deliberate sabotage with devastating results—two murders, and my sight gone."

Libby didn't move a muscle, but the shocking revelation had turned her eyes an inky purple color.

"Your arrival on my doorstep has complicated things because you could be used as a target, as well. It's truly unfortunate that Martin called Dr. Stillman to check on my status this morning and found out my wife had arrived on the scene. The news is all over Nairobi by now. The damage is done. If I know you, you've already seen the back bedroom. Someone set fire to the farmhouse the night before our wedding— one of the reasons I had to cancel our honeymoon so abruptly.

"At first, I attributed the fire to a disgruntled orchard worker on a drunken spree—something of that nature—but I didn't want to take any chances of it happening again when I brought you here to live. I'd hoped to have the room completely repaired and the culprit caught. But for some time, we'd been having problems at the mine and that week, they got worse. The rest, you know."

Everything he said made a horrible kind of sense to Libby.

"Whenever there's a mine disaster, a board of inquiry meets to investigate. If they can prove negligence, then my company will be dissolved and I'll be barred from ever practicing in Kenya again. News of this sort travels fast. I seriously doubt I'd be given a license to work anywhere on the African continent, especially if I'm blamed for the death of two men."

She heard the deep sigh that emanated from him, and in it, the pathos.

"Waking up blind made me see more clearly than ever that I'm a target. The person responsible must be elated that my sight was taken during that cave-in. But what he—or the group of them—doesn't know, is that I intend to fight them. I have a large company with a big payroll. Hundreds of families are looking to me for their livelihood and I'm not going to let them down if I can help it. This kind of tragedy gives the mining and engineering industry a bad name, particularly in Kenya where mining is at the embryo stage."

Libby studied her husband, spellbound by everything she heard. She'd had no idea...no idea at all....

He stared in her direction, almost as if he could actually see her. "I wish I hadn't married you," he said, and his voice was too hard, too uncompromising for pretense. "I want an annulment as soon as possible. Unfortunately, I need to ask a favor of you first."

Silence pervaded the room for a long moment. His desperate situation shattered all her hopes that they could have a future together. She was too numb to speak.

"Libby?" A tiny nerve leaped at the corner of his mouth.

She sucked in her breath. "You told me not to interrupt." She had the satisfaction of watching his hand tighten into a fist against the wall.

"I phoned Charles Rankin from the hospital as soon as I could think rationally. He's agreed to put his affairs in order and fly down here to represent me."

"Thank God!" Libby blurted out, unable to stop herself. If anyone could help Vance, Charles would be that person. Almost twenty years his senior, Charles made a formidable Queen's Counsel and had served as best man at their small garden wedding.

"Hiring Charles is no guarantee, Libby, but he's the only man I trust to make sense of this nightmare. We've talked constantly on the phone, planning our strategy. But your arrival has changed things considerably." He paused as if searching for the right words. "No one knew of our marriage before the accident, and as I told you, I'd planned to have a formal reception announcing it after we returned from our honeymoon. The accident put an end to that. I didn't want a soul to know I had a wife. Whoever is out to destroy me might use you as a means of getting to me. A wife makes a man vulnerable in a dangerous situation like this. Under the circumstances, I didn't want you anywhere near me, for your own sake and mine."

Libby understood so much now—so much. Unable to remain in a seated position any longer, she rose to her feet. "Did you explain all this in the letter?"

"In essence, yes."

"In other words, my coming has put another whip in their hand." Her voice caught. She needed time to sort everything out, to look at the situation from this new perspective.

He rubbed his neck. "Exactly. And after you went to sleep last night, I phoned Charles to let him know you'd come. He agrees with me that the proverbial cat is out of the bag. He feels we have to change tactics."

What was he saying? Libby held her breath.

"If you go back to London now, you might make matters worse. A wife who would run at the first sign of trouble could harm my image with the officials investigating the disaster. Not only that, a united front would instill confidence in the families who rely on me for their living. A wife has a softening influence—a subtle form of power—but it works." His lips twisted almost menacingly.

"I didn't mean to compound your problems."

He shifted in his chair and sat forward. "What's done is done. However, we do have a slight edge. No one knows I suspect foul play except for Charles. If the enemy can be kept in the dark a little longer while Charles does some snooping on his own, it might work to my advantage." His fingers curled around the knife handle. "It would mean pretending to settle down to wedded bliss. I'm to act the part of the besotted bridegroom in public. Everyone will believe that I haven't a care in the world...not with a beautiful new wife in my arms to keep me fully occupied."

When we both know the idea is abhorrent to you.
His behavior in front of Martin Dean was no longer a
mystery.

"We would have a marriage in name only, Libby.
But no one in the world would know that, except for
us. And Charles, of course."

"Of course." The bitterness rose in her throat like
gall.

His dark eyes narrowed pensively. "I wouldn't ask
this of you, but other lives are involved. I can't even
give you a timetable. Charles will be flying in some
time next week. He'll be our houseguest both here at
the farm and at the flat."

"I see." Libby stared straight ahead, seeing nothing.

"More than a few eyebrows would lift if I put in an
appearance at the office this week with you living here
at the farm. Martin knows we're alone, and by the
tone of his voice, I could tell what an impact you made
on him. He's not usually so quiet. He told me that if I
had any brains at all, I'd just hibernate here with you.
In about an hour, everyone at the office will have
heard that I'm enjoying my honeymoon. But the de-
cision is yours." He inhaled sharply. "Is it too much
to ask, Libby?"

Yes! she wanted to shout at the top of her lungs.
Vance sat there within touching distance—the gift
without the giving. How could she bear it? Did she
love him enough to sacrifice her own needs? To put his
above all other considerations? Her lips trembled as
she attempted to find the words. Hadn't she wanted to
be his wife under any and all circumstances? Were the
fates mocking her now?

Libby looked over at the man who held her heart in the palm of his hand. Emotion swelled within her breast at his dark, brooding expression. Wasn't it possible that in time, living together as husband and wife would break down his resistance? He'd loved her enough to marry her. She knew that beyond any doubt.

Libby moistened her lips nervously. "I realize you have an entire company to consider. Now that you've explained everything, of course I want to help."

"Thank you, Libby." His chest heaved with what she felt to be relief. "I'll take every conceivable precaution to protect you. As soon as you're free to return to London, I'll make this up to you."

It was on the tip of her tongue to tell him there was only one way he could do that. "If it's all right with you, I'd like to shower and change. It'll take me the rest of the day to unpack."

He stood up. "This is your home for the time you're here. Do whatever you please. It's not necessary to ask my permission. There's only one more thing I'll ask of you."

Libby's head came up as he reached into his shirt pocket. "It's vital that we make our marriage look as real as possible. I'll have to ask you to wear these rings for a while longer." He put them on the table. "If you need me, I'll be in the library on the phone." He left the kitchen, feeling along the wall as he went.

The amethyst caught the sun and acted as a prism, throwing tiny rainbows onto the ceiling. Now she understood why Vance had held her left hand during the ride to the farm. He didn't dare let on to Martin the true state of affairs between them.

Libby stretched out her hand and slid the rings back in place. She'd bitterly regretted her thoughtless action of the night before. If she had her way, they'd never leave her finger again.

After doing the dishes, she hurried to the bathroom off their bedroom and took a quick shower. The fixtures were new and gleamed a spotless white. It occurred to her again that her husband had performed a minor miracle here in the remote highlands.

She dried herself with a fluffy towel in her favorite periwinkle color and slipped into jeans and a cotton sweater. To keep the hair out of her eyes, she brushed it to one side and braided it with deft fingers, tossing it over her shoulder. She spent part of the afternoon emptying suitcases, hanging clothes in the closet and putting her toiletries in the bathroom.

With her personal unpacking taken care of, Libby headed for the kitchen to prepare a special dinner. There was a certain comfort in knowing that Vance was just a few rooms away instead of thousands of miles away on another continent. What Vance had told her made her want to be within touching distance every second.

In her opinion, Charles couldn't get here fast enough. Vance needed help desperately. She was glad he had the support of Martin Dean, but it crossed her mind to wonder why he'd made no mention of Peter Fromms, another company executive. Their friendship went back to their university days. Once, in London, Libby had met Peter at a party given at the Anson home. She had the impression, then, that the two men were close. And yet, Vance had asked Charles to be his best man. When Libby questioned his choice, she'd been told that Peter couldn't get away. The vague answer hadn't satisfied her, but she'd been too busy to worry about it. Perhaps now that they were settled in at the farm, she could find the appropriate moment to ask Vance about Peter.

Deciding that their first dinner alone warranted something special, she put on a lightweight yellow linen dress, and wore her hair flowing over one shoulder. For an added touch, she put on the gold earrings Vance had given her the year before. Though he couldn't see her, she felt better getting dressed up, and dabbed on some Madame Rochas as a finishing touch.

"Vance? Dinner's ready."

He sat in a swivel chair at a large desk, speaking into a Dictaphone. He switched it off at the sound of her voice and turned in her direction. "I'm not up to much where food is concerned. You go ahead without me."

"It's a light quiche and salad. You need a break," she persisted.

He rubbed his eyes with the palms of his hands. He looked drained. "I'm waiting for an important call."

"You can take it in the kitchen. The quiche is coming out of the oven now, so don't be too long." She turned on her heel and walked through the living room, listening for his footsteps as she entered the kitchen.

A tossed green salad with vinaigrette dressing stood ready in the refrigerator. She'd found a bottle of imported Riesling on one of the shelves and put it on ice for the occasion. After taking the quiche from the oven, she stepped outside to gather a mass of wildflowers. She arranged them with unconscious artistry in a blue and white porcelain bowl—part of a collection Vance had purchased with the farm.

Minutes went by. The lightheartedness she'd felt earlier while preparing their dinner dissipated as she began eating her salad, still alone at the table.

Vance's sudden appearance in the kitchen caused her heart to race out of rhythm. He'd decided to join her, and it was all she could do not to jump up and throw herself in his arms.

"You've put flowers on the table. I detect salvia," he said, sitting down in the same chair he'd used at lunch. His hair looked disheveled, as if he'd run his hands through it many times.

"Mmm. And dahlias, petunias, stocks and sweet canna. Oh, Vance, there's a perfect place to grow herbs outside the kitchen window. It's delightful."

"You sound happy, Libby," he murmured, picking up his fork. A troubled look marred his intelligent face.

"Why wouldn't I be? You've made the farm breathtaking. No wonder you never wanted to come back to England. The fragrance from the blossoms is heavenly. I can't wait to explore the property. Let's go riding first thing in the morning."

"That's impossible." He swallowed his first bite of quiche.

"I don't see why. Dr. Stillman said you were totally fit and that you could take up your usual activities. Besides, Diablo must have missed you these past few weeks, and I'm sure he needs the exercise."

His mouth tightened into a thin line. "My farm manager takes care of the livestock, Libby." That shuttered look was back. "If you're so anxious to get out in the open, take the Jeep and drive along the access roads through the orange groves. You can see a great deal that way."

"I'd prefer to ride. If it's all right with you, I'll saddle Diablo."

"Diablo is too spirited, even for you."

"Then ride double with me. We've done it dozens of times. Just a slow walk around the property. Surely that's not too much to ask."

There was a sustained silence before he reached for his wineglass and sniffed the bouquet. "I didn't know I had any wine in stock," he commented, ignoring her plea about riding.

"I found it while I was putting away the groceries. I wanted this to be a kind of celebration. Our first dinner alone in our new home."

A dark flush stained his hard cheekbones. "As I told you earlier, you have a talent for cooking. Everything is delicious, as usual."

"Thank you." She pushed away her half-empty plate. "Would you like to listen to some music after dinner? I brought a new recording of the Brahms First Piano Concerto with me. I think you'll like Graffman's interpretation."

"Not tonight, Libby."

She excused herself from the table. "What would you like for dessert?" she countered on a lighter tone. "A fig? Or a mango?"

"Nothing for me."

Her eyes went to his empty coffee cup. She reached for the pot and went over to his place to refill it. Inadvertently, her leg brushed against his arm at the same moment that her hair trailed across his cheek. She heard his quick intake of breath before he unexpectedly got to his feet, throwing his napkin on the table. It took the empty wineglass with it.

"Good night," he muttered. In his haste to get away from her, his shoulder bumped against the doorjamb. Several well-chosen epithets escaped before he disappeared from view.

Later, after the dishes were done, Libby walked past the library. As she feared, the sofa bed that stood opposite his desk had been made up; perhaps the farm manager had helped him with it. Vance was already huddled under the blankets and if he wasn't asleep, he pretended to be. She tiptoed down the hall to their bedroom and prepared for bed. Would he ever relent and let her help him relax... let her give him the comfort she craved to shower on him? Hot tears drenched the pillow. What irony that after waiting almost three years to become his wife, she now lay alone in his bed, feeling more empty, more lost, than she'd ever felt in her life....

CHAPTER FOUR

A KNOCK ON THE BEDROOM DOOR awakened Libby from a sound sleep. A glance at her bedside clock said it was after 10 a.m. She couldn't believe she'd slept so late and sat up in the bed, pushing her hair out of her eyes. "Vance? Do you need something?"

"I'm sorry to disturb you," he said through the partially open door, "but since I'm leaving in a few minutes for the rest of the day, I didn't want you waking up, wondering where I'd gone."

Libby shot out of bed and hurried over to the door, opening it wider. "I thought you didn't want to be seen at the office."

"I'm not going to Nairobi."

"Where then?"

"If you must know, I'm going to pay a visit to the families of the two men who were killed during the mine collapse. I couldn't go to their funerals. They live in a Bantu village farther up the escarpment."

"How will you get there?"

"By car, naturally." His mocking voice hinted at a sense of humor that had been buried since the accident.

"I mean, who's driving?"

"James, my farm manager."

"Let me drive you there instead."

"No, Libby. I told you before. I want you to keep a low profile until an arrest is made."

"Surely there can't be any harm in going with you? Mightn't it look better if we were together while you visit the bereaved families? You told me a wife gives you more credibility. And if people in your company already know that I'm here, it might seem odd if I didn't go with you. Please, Vance. I want to get out and see something of the country while I'm here," she added on a sudden burst of inspiration. "What could it hurt?"

He had the harassed look of a man who'd reached the end of his patience. "I need to go right away. Rain is forecast for later in the day, and once it starts, the track into the village becomes a swamp."

"I can be ready in five minutes."

He raked a bronzed hand through his hair. "Better bring a sweater. The air gets cooler the higher we go, particularly when mist accompanies the rain."

She closed her eyes, inordinately pleased that Vance had agreed to take her with him. She resolved not to keep him waiting any longer than necessary. "I'll hurry."

"I've made coffee and toast. Better eat something, first. While you're doing that, I'll have James bring the Jeep around the front."

Her eyes rested on his retreating back. In khaki shirt and trousers, his lean, bronzed body looked more appealing than ever. She assumed the farm manager had assisted him in getting dressed. Libby wondered how long Vance could go before he'd be forced to ask her for help, but she'd worry about that another day.

After a quick shower, she put on jeans and a pale blue blouse with collar and cuffs. Her Scandinavianknit sweater would do as a wrap. With so little time to get ready, Libby left her hair loose, only brushing it until it fell about her shoulders. She'd apply lipstick after breakfast.

The same kind of fluffy white clouds she'd seen yesterday dotted the blue sky as she maneuvered the Jeep along the farm road to the paved highway twenty minutes later. She was used to driving Land Rovers and trucks with trailers on the stud farm, and the Jeep held no mysteries for her. Fortunately, Vance didn't seem to be nervous, and this in turn made her relax. She imagined he had much weightier matters on his mind.

"Do we turn left now, Vance?"

He nodded. "Follow the road for approximately nineteen miles, until you come to a three-way stop. At that point I'll give you further directions. How's the fuel?"

"It says full."

"Good. Let's go."

She saw more of the same scenery they'd passed yesterday, miles of evergreen forests, interspersed by patches of grass, stretching in every direction. So far, there were no humans in sight. Libby felt a sense of isolation that made her thankful to be enclosed in the car with her husband. She had a healthy regard for adventure, but she was in Africa, and it wasn't like driving from London to Hammersmith. Vance would know what to do if she came up against a problem— like a mother lion searching the bush for her lost cubs. She'd heard of things like that happening to tourists out in the high country. But with Vance, she could face anything. The fact that he was blind didn't change that. If only he understood . . .

They'd traveled about ten miles along the highway when Libby became aware of a noise that sounded like thunder. Vance must have guessed her thoughts, because he turned his head toward her. "Don't be alarmed. A herd of gazelles grazes along this side of the forest. Besides zebras, they're the animals you're most likely to see on this trip."

Libby expelled a sigh. "Anything else I need to know about?"

The ghost of a smile hovered on his well-formed lips. "I doubt we'll run into any lions or cheetahs in this neck of the woods. They prefer the dry thorn-bush country. If you want to see that sort of wildlife, you can visit the Masai-Amboseli Game Preserve. It's only a few hours from Nairobi in the opposite direction."

His comments put her at ease, as she knew they were intended to. If she'd obeyed her impulses right then, she'd have stopped the car to make love to him. But she also knew that if she initiated anything, it would backfire on her and she didn't want to ruin this outing.

By the time they reached the spot Vance had told her about, Libby could see a little higher up the escarpment. The forest thinned out to a stand of bamboo and beyond that, moorland. She noticed a distinct drop in the temperature, not only from the thinner air, but because the clouds were clustering in preparation for a storm.

"If you look carefully, Libby, you'll see a track running between the road we're on and the road turning left. Follow it straight into the forest. It winds for about five miles and comes into a clearing filled with huts."

Libby hadn't noticed the track until Vance pointed it out to her. "Should we put the Jeep in four-wheel drive?"

"Not necessary at this point."

Libby started the Jeep again and crossed the highway onto the grassy track, which was little more than a trail, barely discernible through the dense evergreens. With the sun hidden behind clouds, the forest was so dark, it felt like evening.

"Tell me about the men who were killed."

Vance shifted his weight on the seat. "They were hardworking family men who were originally herdsmen from the Bantu tribe. When I opened up the Naivasha mine, they came to work for me. Kenya often experiences seasons of drought, and this forces the men to look for other jobs.

"These two decided to learn the mining business and stayed with it because it meant a steady income and medical care for their families, plus a pension plan. The reason I'm visiting their wives today is to express my condolences, and also to explain that the company will fully support them."

Libby eyed Vance thoughtfully. He would be generous; she knew that about him. The fact that someone apparently harbored jealousy over Vance's success was still incredible to her. She prayed that whoever was responsible for the cave-in would soon be caught.

As Vance had indicated, the track ended in a clearing with about two dozen huts. A group of children dressed in bright cotton shorts and dresses caught sight of the Jeep and ran toward it.

"*Jambo!*" Vance called to them from the open window and they conversed back and forth with him in Swahili.

"What are you saying to them?"

"I've told the children why I've come and asked them to tell the women. They're shy. It's better to let them make the first move."

Libby watched in fascination as the children ran off and talked among themselves. It didn't take long before they were back, the oldest boy, about twelve years of age, acting as spokesman. Another long conversation followed. Vance frowned and Libby could tell immediately that something was wrong.

"What is it, Vance?"

He rubbed his chin. "They say I'm not welcome here. The women won't talk to a...murderer. I was afraid this might happen. As far as they're concerned, anything to do with me or my company brings death."

"Do they speak English?"

Vance nodded.

"Then maybe the women would talk to me. Do they know you lost your sight in that accident? It could make all the difference in how they feel."

"Forget that tack, Libby."

"Vance, don't you see? They're grieving, and they would understand that I, too, am in pain. We share a common bond. Perhaps if they realized that, they'd listen to you. It's worth a try."

"I shouldn't have brought you with me." He slapped his leg in exasperation. "You're my wife. So as far as they're concerned, you bring bad luck, too."

"Not if I have anything to say about it. Vance, you came here to try to comfort these people. Let's not leave until we've exhausted every possibility."

In a lightning move, he reached out his hand and grasped her wrist. "Look, Libby. These women are feeling hostile at the moment. You have no knowledge of their ways and beliefs. I refuse to put you in a potentially explosive situation.''

His grip tightened, and she put her other hand on top of his. "At least ask the children if the women would be willing to talk to me. All they can say is no."

Tension filled the silence as he let go of her wrist and pulled away from the hand that had been caressing his. After a few seconds, he said something else to the children and they ran off. Neither he nor Libby spoke while they waited.

It wasn't long before the children all came back one more time. The spokesman pointed to Libby. "You can go. But not him."

"I don't like this, Libby. I'd rather you didn't do it.''

Her heart pounded hard. "I want to. I admit I'm nervous, but I have an idea how those women feel."

His face wore a haunted expression. "At the first sign of trouble, you start screaming and don't stop."

"I promise." She slid out of the Jeep before he could change his mind and followed the children to a hut near the edge of the forest.

As she walked around to the entrance, a woman in a flowered dress stepped out, holding a baby, with a toddler clutching her skirt. Another woman stood in the doorway. Their dark eyes stared at her without the slightest glimmer of welcome. Libby felt no fear, only sorrow that they'd lost their husbands. Vance, after all, was still alive....

"I'm Libby Anson," she began, putting her hands in her back pockets.

They said nothing. She cleared her throat.

"I know your men are gone, and nothing can bring them back, but my husband wants you to know that the company will pay your support for as long as you live."

The women simply stood there. She had no idea if she was getting through to them.

"It's true that my husband is still alive, but the accident hurt him, too. He can't see anymore, and because he can't see, he doesn't think he's a man. And because he doesn't think he's a man, he wants to send me away. I want to stay because I love him the way you loved your husbands."

The women in the doorway took a step closer.

Libby took a deep breath and went on. "My husband's suffering, and if you would let him help you, it would help him. He couldn't come to see you before now because he just left the hospital yesterday. First thing this morning, he told me he wanted to come here to see you, to make sure you were all right—to tell you not to worry about money."

"Some people say the accident happened because of him," the woman nearest Libby said in a slow, measured voice.

"Does it make sense he would cause an accident that would leave him blind?" Libby reasoned, staring at the woman until she averted her eyes. "He's trying to find out who caused the accident, and when he does, that person will be punished."

"Where are your babies?" the other woman asked shyly.

Libby swallowed hard. "As long as my husband is worried about you and his company, there will be no babies."

The two women looked at each other, then back at Libby. "You want babies?"

"Very much," came her heartfelt reply. "I want sons and daughters as fine as yours."

"Your husband cannot see your eyes?"

"No. Everything is like night."

"You don't need to see to make babies." The other woman smiled as she spoke.

"You're right, but Mr. Anson is a proud man. Do you know what that means?"

Both women nodded. One of them said, "When my husband did not come back with meat from the hunt, he ran off for three days. I could not find him anyplace."

The three women gazed at one another with understanding.

"Mr. Anson is out in the car. He'd like to tell you these things himself, if you would follow me." Without waiting to see whether they did, Libby walked back to the Jeep. Vance stood in front of the hood, his arms folded across his chest, waiting.... A reassuring sight.

"It's all right, Vance," she murmured, wrapping her hand around his upper arm. Some of the rigidity left his body when she touched him. He unexpectedly put an arm around her shoulders.

The two women weren't far behind. They spoke to him in Swahili, sounding reserved at first, but he answered them warmly and a long conversation took place. Libby needed no translator. Everything Vance felt was expressed in his eyes and his gestures. He pulled two envelopes out of his breast pocket and urged them to take the money. After a slight hesita-

tion, they accepted his offering, then grew more animated.

Vance's hand tightened on Libby's shoulder. "They
seem very taken with you, and they've invited us to
stay for a meal. We can't refuse," he muttered beneath his breath so only Libby could hear. "Taste
everything offered."

Something in his manner told her she was in for a
few surprises and that he found the situation amus-
ing. She slid her arm around his waist. "I'll eat everything you eat."

Together they walked to a cleared space outside the
huts, which appeared to be the communal dining area.
Long poles were crisscrossed over an open fire, and a
baglike holder hung suspended above the flame.

Vance planted himself on the hard-packed earth and
pulled Libby down beside him. Wooden plates and
implements were soon placed in front of them, the
plates filled with various foods that Libby found totally unrecognizable but quite edible. On her first try,
she thought the meal tasted something like cornmeal,
sweet potatoes and rubbery chicken. Best of all,
everything was hot, and the fire felt good. The sky
looked ever more threatening as giant thunderheads
moved swiftly overhead, ushering in a cold wind. The
children seemed impervious to the chill.

"We've got to get out of here, Libby. I can smell
rain in the air." She and Vance finished their food and
as politely as they could explained that they needed to
leave before the storm hit. They thanked their host-
esses profusely, then hurried back to the Jeep.

The first drops of rain spattered the windshield as
Libby started the motor. The downpour began in earnest before she'd gone a mile. Vance hadn't exagger-

ated. Beneath the sparse grass oozed thick, slippery mud, several inches deep. To Libby it felt like driving on a skating rink, particularly since they were on a decline all the way to the main road. It was all she could do to keep the Jeep from veering sideways off the track.

"I can't seem to control the car." Libby could hear the panic in her voice.

"In that case, slowly pull over to the side and turn off the motor. We'll wait for the cloudburst to pass."

"I'll try," she said unsteadily, but when she started to do as he suggested, the Jeep turned a half circle. In her effort to right the car, she overcorrected, sending them over the side of the track.

"Vance! We're going to crash!" A split second before the impact, Libby felt his arms enfold her shoulders, shielding her face. She waited for the splintering of glass and crunch of metal, but all she heard was the soft brush of pine needles against the body of the car. The rain came down harder.

"We're all right, Libby," he murmured in husky tones, pressing feverish kisses on the side of her neck, crushing her close to him until her shivering stopped. "Just well and truly wedged in a copse of pines."

A shudder racked her body and she clung to him. "I've never been so frightened in my life. The wheel spun right out of my hand."

"Shh." He lowered his mouth to hers. "It's over. Don't think about it." And then he was kissing her with such hunger it was impossible not to respond. The accident had set their emotions at a pitch. Libby couldn't get enough of him as one kiss became another. The ecstasy of being in his arms like this surpassed her daydreams and even her memories.

Hardly conscious of what she was doing, Libby's hand slipped inside his shirt, seeking the warmth of hair-roughened skin. "I love you," she whispered, covering his face and eyelids with kisses.

Suddenly he expelled a long breath and sat back in the bucket seat, putting her gently but firmly away from him. "You seem to be fully recovered from our little mishap. I'm going to get out—try to tell how far down we're mired."

Libby needed the few minutes that he was outside to pull herself together. Being so rudely transported back to reality was more shocking than the accident had been. Perhaps he'd only intended to comfort her, but the raw passion of his kisses set her aflame. The strong physical attraction had always been there, from the moment they met, but now it was like a conflagration. If he touched her one more time, she felt as if she'd go up in smoke.

THE RAIN STILL CAME DOWN steadily as Vance climbed into the Jeep. He shrugged out of his parka and tossed it in the rear, then wiped his muddy hands on the paper tissues Libby gave him. "We're stuck here until the rain stops. When you can see to back out, I'll push. I think we'll be able to get ourselves up to the road without too much trouble. As far as I can tell, nothing is broken or even badly damaged."

"How long do you think it will rain?"

"Not much longer, but while we're waiting, we might as well get comfortable. Turn on the ignition and I'll switch on the heater."

It wasn't long before the interior of the Jeep was warm and cozy. Vance reached around the back of her seat and rummaged for a satchel on the floor. He opened it and pulled out a bottle of brandy.

"Behold—my first-aid kit, but this is one of the rare times I've had to use it." He felt for the glove compartment and lifted out a thermos, unscrewing the cup. "Would you like a drink?" He carefully poured the brandy, spilling only a few drops, and offered her the first sip.

It was on the tip of her tongue to refuse, but she changed her mind. She had to do something to counteract his nearness. "Thank you." The fiery spirits burned their way down her throat and she coughed.

When she handed him the cup, he quickly finished off what he'd poured. Then, far too soon for her liking, he poured himself another drink. Vance was normally a temperate man, and it surprised her to see that he intended to get drunk. There was no other explanation.

Some time later, she realized that the rain had stopped. She'd been so busy observing her husband's behavior, she hadn't noticed. "Vance?"

"Mmm?"

"Shall we try to get ourselves out now? It's not raining anymore."

"In a minute."

"But it's getting late. It'll be dark soon."

"It's always dark," his voice slurred. "Don't be afraid."

She took a deep breath. "I'm never afraid with you."

"Then you sure as hell should be." On that note, he made himself more comfortable and fell asleep with his head against the window.

Not knowing whether to laugh or cry, Libby rested her head on the back of the seat. Today's experience had shown her yet another side of her husband. If loving him meant spending the night in a muddy bog in the highlands of Kenya, so be it. He couldn't ignore her presence indefinitely. There had to come a time when he'd lower his defenses, and she planned to be there, waiting. She turned her head to look at him. Little by little, her eyelids drooped.

The next thing she knew, Vance was shaking her awake. "Libby?"

She lifted her head, surprised to discover she'd been asleep against his shoulder. A huge white moon had appeared over the top of the escarpment. No trace of clouds remained.

"What time does my watch say?"

She rubbed her eyes and sat up. "Ten forty-five."

He muttered something unintelligible beneath his breath. "I apologize for passing out on you like that."

"It's all right."

"No, it isn't," he snapped, his voice sharp with self-loathing. "I should be getting down on my knees to you for smoothing the way with those women today. That took courage." He reached behind him for his parka and opened the door. "Put it in reverse, and when I say go, press the accelerator. The mud's a little firmer now, and we just might be able to perform the required miracle." After a dozen tries, Vance managed to shove the Jeep over the lip of the track. He jumped inside, almost insultingly enthusiastic to be free of their predicament. "Let's go home."

Home. Whether it was a slip of the tongue or not, Libby obeyed his edict with the greatest of pleasure.

CHAPTER FIVE

THE FIRST WEEK PASSED swiftly as Libby settled into a routine at the farm. By tacit agreement, Vance didn't go into the Nairobi office. He ate breakfast with Libby and they listened to the news over the radio. Then Vance spent the rest of the day with his farm manager, coming home only for lunch. Libby, in turn, did the laundry, cleaned the house and made preparations for dinner. She treasured her evenings with Vance the most.

Vance would come in, shower and change. They'd enjoy a sherry on the *stoep*, then eat dinner together. Sometimes they spent the evening quietly, listening to classical music; other nights the conversation was intellectual and stimulating...and impersonal. They talked about everything except themselves, their feelings, their future. But it was a start; Libby knew that. And anyone seeing them would have assumed they'd settled down to wedded bliss. No one could guess that intimacy between them—the intimacy afforded by marriage—was nonexistent.

Since that night in the forest, Vance had made every effort to keep physical as well as emotional distance between them. And Libby knew that as soon as he started putting in full days at the office, the nature of their time together would change once again. Not only would he be burdened with worry over the board of inquiry findings, but once Charles arrived, Libby doubted she and Vance would have any time alone at all.

Libby awakened Sunday morning with the realization that this was his last day at home before he would be going into the office again. She'd asked him to meet her at the stable to go riding, but he'd made some noncommittal answer, dashing her hopes that they'd spend part of the day together.

She put on jeans and a cotton-knit sun top, deciding that she'd go riding alone. After a light breakfast of juice and toast, she set out for the barn. If Vance was up and about, she had no way of knowing without peeking into the library, and she'd long since given up that ritual. He almost bit her head off if he thought she was checking up on him.

The days were growing warmer and more beautiful and there wasn't a cloud in sight. She found Diablo in the end stall. Two plow horses munching on fresh hay stood docilely in the other stalls. One of the farm workers must have been up early to muck out the barn, then feed and water the animals. Delightedly, Libby breathed in the familiar scents of horses and leather and hay. She felt a sharp stab of longing for her own horse, King, but thrilled to the idea of a ride on Vance's stallion.

He whinnied at her approach and began to sniff her as she entered his stall. She spoke gently to him, rubbing his nose and forelock. "Well, Diablo. It's been a long time, you beauty. Want to go for a ride? Vance doesn't think I can handle you, but we know better, don't we?"

A bridle hung on the wall. She removed it and slipped the bit into the horse's mouth. Once that was accomplished, she led him out of the stall. He seemed gentler than she'd ever seen him as she walked him into the sunlight.

"I thought I made it clear that you were never to ride Diablo alone, Libby!"

She whirled around to see him standing near the barn entrance with his hand on the door frame. Her eyes took in the fit of his knit shirt and the jeans that he wore with a careless elegance. For want of a better word, Vance was a beautiful man. The lines and planes of his classic bone structure drew her gaze, as always, but this morning, his strong jawline looked more prominent than usual. "I hoped you'd be here. Diablo came right to me. . . . He knew my voice immediately. You can tell he's dying for a romp. Won't you take a short ride with me?"

"I don't seem to have a choice." Diablo could scent his master, and wandered over to nuzzle Vance's broad chest. Libby envied the horse that much freedom where Vance was concerned. He talked to Diablo in soothing tones, then mounted him with a grace and agility Libby could scarcely believe. He held out his left hand. "Come on up, Libby."

The world stood still for a second as she experienced that feeling of déjà vu. A tremor passed through her body as she grasped his proffered hand and swung herself on Diablo's back so that she sat in front of Vance. They'd often ridden bareback together. Vance had always insisted on it, wanting her so close they rode as one, whispering that he never wanted anything to separate them.

Diablo pranced in place, anxious to enjoy his morning jaunt. Vance's strong arms came around her waist. Libby let herself lean back against his chest where she could feel his heartbeat. A mixture of emotions swept over her. Excitement...elation... tenderness. Love, for this man whose courage was tested every minute of every day. She closed her eyes, trying to imagine how it would feel to be blind as she sat astride Diablo. "Where shall we go first?"

"Ride into the sun," he suggested and patted Diablo's flank. As if sensing that he carried precious cargo, the stallion walked along the access paths at a gentle pace. The farm lay nestled in a valley closely cultivated with orange trees. The endless dips and rises of the hillocks in the background were a constant source of enchantment to Libby. She and Vance cantered past new groves of peach, plum and pear trees, laden with heavy blossoms that gave off an intoxicating perfume.

Diablo seemed to feel a sense of freedom as they left the orchards. He picked up his pace and they began a rhythmic gallop through the grass, swerving around the evergreens. The stallion responded instantly to Vance's lightest touch, his softest commands. Libby simply held the reins and rested against her husband. Although they'd ridden like this many times before, Libby had never felt such a heightened awareness of the world around her. But then, White Oaks in England was tame by comparison. To be this close to Vance in the land he'd adopted for his own could only add to her wonder.

Much later, Vance reined in Diablo until they proceeded at a leisurely walk. Until now, neither of them had felt the urge to speak. She knew Vance was starting to enjoy himself from the way his body relaxed. The ride had been so exhilarating, she'd forgotten that her husband couldn't see and wondered if he'd suffered many moments of unease while they'd been galloping.

"What's it like to fly straight into the wind now?" she asked, turning her head to one side to ask her question. She inadvertently grazed his hard jaw with her lips and felt the shudder that passed through his body. She hadn't meant to be provocative, having endured his anger and worse, his rejection, too often since he'd left the hospital in Nairobi. Every time he flinched at her nearness, she was wounded a little more. "Vance?" she prompted, her face staring ahead as she fought to keep her voice steady.

"If you're asking me if being blind makes this different from the last time we rode together, the answer is no. I couldn't see anything then, either—not with this profusion of black silk impairing my vision," he responded in a lazy drawl that sent her pulses racing crazily. "I'm glad you haven't cut it, or changed perfumes. It's nice to know some things stay the same." His voice had a husky timbre she hadn't heard in a long time, and she felt herself go limp with desire.

Diablo came to a standstill near a cluster of trees, apparently content to nibble on the sweet grass. Vance raised his face to the sky, then took a deep breath. "I can tell by the position of the sun that we've been out a long time. We'd better head back. I'm expecting some calls around lunchtime."

Inside, Libby rebelled. "It's still fairly early in the day. Would you mind if we dismounted for a few minutes? I need to stretch."

Vance went quiet for a moment. "You're not feeling ill, are you?" His tone was laced with concern, an encouraging sign that he wasn't as indifferent to her as he pretended to be. She didn't want this morning to end, knowing he'd shut himself away in the library as soon as they returned, and she wouldn't see him the rest of the day.

"I've never felt better, but I haven't ridden for a while and my leg muscles are a little sore."

She could feel his breath catch in irritation, but he said nothing. The next thing she knew, he'd dismounted. She looked down at her husband, loving him more at this moment than ever before. He lifted his arms—almost impatiently, she guessed—to help her to the ground.

Perhaps it was the brilliance of his velvet-brown eyes, or the need to be in his arms. Whatever it was, in her haste to reach him, she swung her leg over Diablo with too much vigor. The momentum sent her flying headlong against Vance. The impact caused both of them to go sprawling into the grass, forcing a groan from Vance's throat.

"Vance!" she screamed in alarm, getting to her knees. She leaned over him, cradling his face in her hands. The soft earth had cushioned his fall, but he'd taken the brunt of her weight and had somehow struck his head against a protruding rock when he went down, dazing himself.

"Darling?" The endearment slipped out. "Are you all right? Please...please be all right." She choked on a sob as the tears streamed down her cheeks. She ran gentle hands through his dark brown hair and discovered a small lump already forming near his right temple. He still hadn't opened his eyes, but to her relief he seemed to be breathing normally.

"It was my fault," she moaned, her chest heaving. "Vance," she cried out, covering his face in featherlight kisses, trying to give comfort in the only way she knew how. Her horror increased when she realized the injury had happened on the same side of his head as the earlier one. "Wake up, Vance. Please wake up." Her selfish desires had brought him to this, she agonized inwardly. They were so far away from the farmhouse, without a soul in sight.

"Libby?" His hands lifted to her bare arms and he kneaded them in slow, deliberate movements. She raised her head from his neck, which was wet from her tears. His half-veiled eyes seemed to see right through her as she stared down at him. "Are you hurt?" he fired the question. "Tell me the truth!"

She could hardly believe his anxiety for her safety. "I'm fine, Vance." She swallowed hard. "You're the one who's hurt! There's a swelling on the side of your head, near your injury. It's my fault—I tried to dismount in too big a hurry."

A flash of anger hardened his expression as he became fully aware of his surroundings. "Tell me the truth, Libby. You weren't feeling well a minute ago. Don't pretend with me!"

"I swear I'm not pretending, Vance. I just wanted to give Diablo a rest and exercise my stiff muscles for a minute."

He seemed frantic with concern. "If I could just see for myself that you're telling me the truth." She wasn't prepared for the cursory exploration of her body. His hands felt for her limbs, as if he had to prove to himself that she was in one piece.

"What is this you're wearing?" His hands came in contact with her knitted sun top, and their touch was no longer clinical. This new sensation was so different, a gasp of pleasure escaped her softly parted lips.

He seemed to love the feel of her satiny skin and continued to caress her, feeling her throat and nape till his fingers twisted convulsively in her hair.

"I swore I wasn't going to let this happen," he whispered, but even as he groaned in self-disgust he was drawing her head down to his until their breath mingled. "Libby..." His mouth fastened over hers with an exquisite urgency. He pulled her close and they clung.

The earth reeled away as Libby gave herself up to this long-suppressed passion. There was such profound hunger in the way he took her lips and mouth over and over again. She felt boneless, weightless, delirious with longing. His mouth ignited needs inside Libby that took on a life of their own.

Heart and mind were his to mold into anything he wanted. Libby was a writhing, breathless supplicant craving assuagement only he could give. She was far too drugged to hear Diablo's restless pawing a few yards away.

The stallion began snorting and whinnying ferociously. His hooves pounded the grassy turf in a frenzied kind of movement, and the sounds he emitted were eerily human. In that instant, Vance rolled them through the grass with a superhuman strength and speed that robbed her of breath.

"Don't move. Don't make a sound." He put a hand over her mouth. They lay rigid with Libby's head pressed into his chest. He held her in a painful grip, but she welcomed it. Having been around horses all her life, Libby recognized that Diablo was in combat with something hostile, perhaps even lethal. This was a violent, elemental land. She clung all the harder to the tense body shielding her from danger.

At last, when she thought she couldn't bear to be in ignorance any longer, Diablo's convulsive stomping quieted down. Then Libby could hear his gentle neighing and the occasional rush of hot air through his nostrils. Whatever had bothered the big stallion was no longer a threat, and Vance lessened the pressure of his hold.

"Slowly, without making any noise, raise your head, Libby. Peer over my shoulder. Diablo has been tangling with a snake. I heard it hiss seconds before Diablo struck out. Tell me what you can see."

She did as he told her. "You're right. It's a snake." Her voice shook.

"Describe it to me."

Libby licked her lips, which had gone dry. Reaction had set in and her teeth were chattering. "I'm not sure. It—it's about three feet long, with a kind of hood. It's d-dead, I think."

"And the color?"

"I'm not sure. Grayish brown?"

"Just as I thought. Stay where you are." Stealthy as a cat, Vance rose to his haunches and whistled. Diablo whinnied and started toward his master. Awe replaced fear as Libby took in the sight of man and horse in total communion with each other. Vance rose to his feet, speaking to the animal in low tones, patting his fetlock, and smoothing the foam from his great neck. "Climb on Diablo while I continue to gentle him, Libby. He's had quite a fright."

Libby scrambled to her feet and swung herself onto Diablo's slick back. The horse trembled beneath her. Libby's eyes sought out the snake, which lay lifeless in the disturbed grass. She shuddered as if several volts of electricity had just passed through her body. In a flash, Vance levered himself close to her, and once again they moved toward the farmhouse.

"Let's go," he whispered in her ear. He urged the stallion into a full gallop, both of them holding the reins. They slowed to a canter as they reached the first grove of fruit trees.

"I'll tell James about the snake as soon as we get back to the stable. He'll send some of the men out on the property to dispose of it, and see if there are others. I haven't seen a snake here for a couple of years. It's a rare occurrence, Libby. But take this as a warning never to go riding alone. I want your promise on that. A spitting cobra is lethal and aims for the eyes. Its venom can blind a person in just minutes."

Libby felt faint. "I'll never ride without you."

"Then we understand each other."

"Yes."

"Thank God you didn't panic. You're a unique woman, Libby." His voice was gruff with tension, and something like admiration.

"You didn't give me a chance. I wasn't aware of where I was when—I mean..." She floundered for words as the recollection of what had happened earlier came back to thrill her. If Diablo hadn't been frightened by the snake, Vance might have broken down completely and made love to her.

"No explanation is necessary. Forget everything that happened back there, Libby. Because neither incident will happen again. I'll see to it."

His grim avowal plunged her into an abyss that seemed to swallow her alive. She reviewed the events of their ride while she showered and changed clothes. Blind or not, Vance had been in charge from the moment he followed her out to the barn. Surely he could understand that losing his sight hadn't robbed him of his manhood or his ability to protect. On the contrary, his sense of hearing seemed to have automatically become more acute. Libby hadn't even heard the hiss of the snake. It went to prove how well Vance could function in his dark, new world.

The swelling on his head needed attention right away. She opened one of the kitchen cupboards where first-aid supplies were kept and reached for pain tablets and an ice pack, which she quickly filled. "Vance?" She knocked on the library door. "I have something for your head. May I come in?"

"There's no need, Libby."

"Let me be the judge of that." Without waiting another second for his permission, she let herself into the room. He'd obviously just come from the shower. He wore his toweling robe and sat on the edge of the sofa bed.

One black brow lifted sardonically. "Why did you bother to knock?"

She had difficulty believing that he was the same man of a half hour ago, the man who'd started making love to her in the grass—who'd practically devoured her. Her body was still on fire. How could he sit there so calmly, after what had happened between them? "I don't recall hearing you ask my permission before you rolled me away from danger a little while ago. Certain situations dictate how one must act. And looking at the bump on your temple, I know exactly what I'm going to do. Lie down, Vance, and put this pack on your head. I've brought two of the tablets Dr. Stillman prescribed for pain, and I'll get you a glass of water. Take them if you need to. They're right here on this nightstand."

She didn't wait to hear his reaction as she went into the guest bathroom for water. When she returned, she discovered that he'd taken her advice. He lay on top of the bed, holding the ice pack to his temple. His face was a mask of tight lines, and she felt another wrench that she was the person responsible.

"Here's the water." She brushed his hand with the glass. "Take the pills. They'll ease the pain." To her surprise, he reached for the medication and swallowed it without argument, setting the empty glass on the stand without her help. She could detect a distinct pallor beneath his tanned skin and her concern grew. The room felt cool; maybe she ought to cover him with the light cotton blanket that lay across the end of the bed.

"You're hovering, Libby," he muttered while she stood there, racked with indecision. "Let's get it over with. Cover me up and plump the pillows like a dutiful little wife. Play it out to the end."

Her hands went to her hips. Vance was about as helpless as an angry tiger with a thorn in its paw. She spread the blanket over him clumsily, her hands shaking. Whoever said that words can't hurt didn't know what he was talking about! She sucked in her breath and left the room, almost slamming the door. But she didn't want to give Vance that much satisfaction.

Knowing they both needed something substantial, she busied herself in the kitchen making lunch. When it was ready, she went back to his room and found him in a deep sleep. His face had relaxed, but he'd been restless before dropping off. The blanket was twisted about him as if he'd rolled over and over on the bed. She drew closer and discovered that the ice pack had dropped to the floor.

Frowning, Libby bent to pick it up, intending to put it on his temple. As she leaned over, she saw beads of perspiration on his forehead and upper lip. She felt his forehead. He was hot! The touch of her hand should have awakened him, but he slept on. Alarmed, she hurried to the phone to call Dr. Stillman. He finally came on the line after the nursing sister paged him throughout the hospital. Speaking quietly, Libby explained the sequence of events that had caused the lump on his forehead, and the aftermath.

"I don't think it's anything serious, Mrs. Anson," he told her. "I doubt he's suffering from anything more than a slight concussion. He hasn't vomited. A nasty bump on the head will naturally produce swelling, even nausea and fever. You've done the right thing. But to ease your mind and mine, check on him at odd intervals during the next twelve hours to see if his breathing is normal. If he sleeps too much, or his sleep isn't natural, call me—day or night. And I want to see him at the hospital in the morning. All right?"

"Thank you, doctor. I'll make sure he's there." He rang off as she replaced the receiver. Knowing she couldn't concentrate on anything else with Vance in this condition, Libby took her sandwich into Vance's room, and chose a thriller from his bookshelves. She'd be able to read and watch for changes in him at the same time. The book absorbed her for about forty-five minutes, but she heard Vance stir, and put it down. He came fully awake and sat up in the bed, rubbing his chin where the beginnings of a beard were visible.

Libby walked over to the bed. His color had improved and she felt great relief. She even thought the swelling had gone down a little. "Are you feeling better?"

"Libby?" he murmured, as if he still needed to get his bearings. "What do you think you're doing in here?" he demanded in a nasty tone of voice.

"You were running a temperature, and when you didn't wake up, I called Dr. Stillman. He—"

"You what?" he thundered, cutting her off.

"Don't be angry, Vance. I had to be absolutely sure I'd done the right thing for you. He wants to see you at the hospital in the morning."

"How dare you take matters into your own hands?" His dark brown eyes glittered with anger.

"I dared because you needed help, and because I'm the one who caused you to fall in the first place."

He got to his feet. "I gave you permission to treat this as your own home. But you have no business interfering with my life, Libby. This room is strictly off limits. I'll make my own doctor's appointments, if and when I need to. Is that clear?" He stomped out of the library and made his way to the bathroom down the hall with few casualties.

"Should I call him back and cancel, or will you? Dr. Stillman expects to hear from one of us."

"Just leave things alone, Libby!" he bellowed. "You've done more than enough already."

Angry enough to shake him, she retraced her steps to the kitchen and put his lunch back in the refrigerator. Needing an outlet to vent her frustration, she gathered up the soiled linen and started a wash. It didn't help. When her gaze happened to light on the Jeep parked in the rear, she didn't hesitate to walk out of the house and go for a drive. Vance made her so furious, she had half a mind to stay out all night. It wouldn't hurt for him to do a little worrying for a change.

She had no idea where she was going...only that the road eventually led to Nairobi. Halfway to the city, she realized that she'd done it again and let Vance get to her.

At the next village, she did an hour's shopping, impulsively stopping to buy fresh pineapple at a roadside stand before turning back toward home. By the time she pulled into the driveway, she felt reasonably calm and in the mood to make fondue *au fromage* for dinner. The Swiss national dish was one of Vance's favorites. They had Kirschwasser and Gruyère cheese on hand. All she needed to do was warm up some French bread. The pineapple would be a wonderful addition to the fruit salad she planned to fix.

"It sounds like you bought out the stores."

Libby turned in the direction of her husband's voice on her third trip to the back porch to collect her purchases. The indulgent tone held no trace of the anger he'd displayed earlier. Apparently the solitude had brought calm to his afternoon. She should have been pleased, but part of her hoped that he'd missed her. Her eyes went swiftly to his temple. Although there was an angry bruise, the swelling had gone down. He'd managed to put on white shorts and a burgundy polo shirt that emphasized his tan.

"I find the native markets irresistible. It's impossible to go into one of those shops and leave without buying anything."

"So I've been told by my impoverished married male acquaintances."

Libby started to laugh and his low chuckle joined hers. "I promise not to put you in the poorhouse yet, but give me a few years."

Until his smile faded, she didn't realize what she'd said. The silence stretched uncomfortably.

"I'll start dinner." She picked up a potted plant in one arm, and a fishnet carryall full of groceries in the other, then headed through the swinging door.

"It's already made."

She could tell that as soon as she stepped into the kitchen. The delicious aroma of potatoes and frying onions wafted past her nostrils. Steaks were ready on the grill and the table was set. Proof of his determination and indomitable will, Libby thought. Out of his anger, *this* was the result. A real step forward.

She put her things on the counter. "I'll go freshen up and join you in a few minutes."

"A martini will be waiting for you on the *stoep* when you're ready."

"That sounds wonderful. I'll hurry."

"Libby—?"

The hesitant tone in his voice caught her off guard and made her a trifle uneasy. "Yes?"

"I'm not unaware of how hard you've been working since we came here. I hadn't intended to saddle you with all the domestic chores, but as I promised when we came here, I'll make this up to you."

"Don't worry about it, Vance. As I've been informed by my bedraggled married female acquaintances, it goes with the territory."

Dinner was a taciturn affair. Vance broke the long silence by offering her more steak.

"I can't eat another bite. I've already had two helpings of everything. You're going to make someone a superb wife, Vance."

"If you're trying to tell me that a blind man has his uses, don't. James did most of the work."

Carefully, she put her coffee cup back on the saucer. "I was thanking you for a delicious dinner, but you wouldn't recognize a compliment if it walked up to you and shook your hand."

"Probably not," came the mocking retort.

Libby pushed herself away from the table. "I'll drive you to work tomorrow. If Charles is going to be staying with us, we need to get one of the bedrooms ready. Do you have a preference for the kind of furniture you'd like in that north bedroom?"

He wiped his mouth with a napkin. "I'll talk to James about arranging for work crews to paint and do repairs. But the furniture is your department. I have an account at Caulder's. You should be able to find whatever you want there, and they'll deliver."

"When I'm through, could we meet for lunch?"

He shook his dark head. "I have a full calendar tomorrow. You drive back to the farm and I'll have one of the men from the office drop me off. It might be late. And just so you'll know, I've opened up an account in your name at Lloyd's. Withdraw whatever funds you need."

She arched one delicate eyebrow. "Aren't you afraid I'll abscond with the lot?" she asked, hoping to recapture that rare moment of humor they'd shared earlier, but a bleakness entered his eyes.

"What I'm really afraid of is that you won't."

Her hands formed into fists. "What's the matter, Vance? Is this mockery of a marriage becoming a little too much to handle? Maybe you need to phone Charles and have another summit meeting. Tell him you're tired of playing the besotted bridegroom. Maybe—"

"That's enough, Libby. I shouldn't have said anything. If you must know, I hate the idea of involving you in this ugly mess...particularly when we don't know what's down the road."

She inhaled deeply. "Does anyone?"

"We're talking about a man or group of men who'll commit murder to get what they want. Not your average household problem."

She got up from the table and started clearing the dishes. "You asked for my help and I agreed. As you told me earlier, your entire company looks to you for leadership. After meeting those women, I understand a great deal more about what's at stake here. I'm not only involved now, I'm committed. And so are you."

Vance rose to his full height. "That may be true, but I intend to keep you on the sidelines. Don't even think of coming into the office. I want you to have low visibility where my staff is concerned. Do your business in Nairobi, then come straight back to the farm. James has been filled in on the situation. He has strict orders to keep watch over you while I'm in the city. If you need to get in touch with me, I've left the phone numbers in the study."

Libby listened with her heart as well as her mind. Her presence had turned into a mixed blessing. She had no intention of adding to his anxieties if she could help it.

Vance frowned and thrust a hand through his hair. "Libby," he said urgently, "I prefer you to stay away from Nairobi as much as possible. I'll have to ask you to drive me to the office occasionally, but I want you to come straight back to the farm. You're much safer here. If I have to be gone overnight, James will leave

Angus, his Great Dane, to stand guard. He and Angus watched the place while I was in the hospital.''

Libby reassured him, promising to be careful and discreet. They agreed that she'd drive him to Nairobi for the next week, taking the opportunity to do as many of the essential errands as she could. When that was settled, Vance left to lie down again, and Libby began to wash their dinner dishes.

As she wiped the counters, she realized how badly she needed someone to talk to. She had no friends here yet, nobody to whom she could unburden herself. Perhaps she'd stop by the hospital after she dropped Vance at his office. Dr. Stillman had mentioned a Mrs. Grady, one of the nursing matrons who worked with blind patients. Maybe this woman could do something or say something that would help Libby get through to Vance. To make him understand that her only thought, her only desire, was to be a real wife to him.

CHAPTER SIX

"TAGGING HIS CLOTHES and shoes is the easy part. But you will have to choose the right way of telling him what you plan to do. No doubt he'll ignore you—or lash out—but give him time."

Libby took a deep breath. "And what about a cane? He's still bumping into things, Mrs. Grady."

"Don't say anything about that, yet. He needs to deal with that when the time's right, probably when he breaks a leg." She laughed at her own joke but Libby couldn't imagine anything worse. "What else is on your mind, Mrs. Anson?" The cheery Englishwoman eyed Libby kindly.

"I wouldn't even know where to begin."

The older woman's face grew pensive. "Then come again the next time you're in Nairobi. I can always fit you in if you're willing to wait."

"Thank you, Mrs. Grady. I might just do that. For the next little while, I'm going to be driving Vance to work every morning. He'll never know if I stop off here occasionally before I go back to the farm."

"I'll be expecting you. And a word of advice, in the meantime. Keep on loving him, the way you have been. It's the best tonic there is."

What else could she do? Libby mused to herself, but she left the nursing station in a lighter mood. Opening up to Mrs. Grady eased the burden a little.

Back at the farm, Libby spent the day in her bedroom, going through a box of photographs she'd brought from England. There were pictures of Vance's mother, dead many years, several of his father in his younger days as an engineer in Kenya working on one of the dams.

She pulled out pictures of her parents, of her natural father, snapshots of her best friends. It took hours to sort them into piles—some to be framed, others to be put in albums. Libby wanted to surround Vance and herself with memories and with the personal touches their new home still lacked.

The next day, she walked through the house jotting down decorating ideas, as the work crews transformed the bedrooms and their cheerful talk brought life to the house. She decided that the elegance of French doors and high ceilings in the living room required a more traditional approach. An exquisite French escritoire and matching side-arm chairs that she'd inherited through her mother's family were in storage in London. She'd send for them, as well as several favorite paintings hanging in her bedroom at home. Those items would serve as a focal point. A few well-chosen pieces of African art would blend nicely with her overall scheme. But she needed Vance's opinion before she started on the dining room.

Wednesday, she ordered the furniture from Caulder's and it arrived two days later. Libby had the twin beds placed in the newly painted bedrooms, then spent most of the day looking for just the right bits and pieces to create a warm, inviting atmosphere.

Except for the brief time together at breakfast and during the drive into Nairobi, Libby saw next to nothing of her husband. Someone on his staff drove him home each night, long after dark. He'd disappear into the library telling Libby not to bother with a meal for him as he'd already eaten.

He seemed more determined than ever to distance himself from her, and this in turn made her more determined to become indispensable to him. But his constant rejection of any overture on her part was wearing her down. Still, Mrs. Grady had told her that in time, this would probably change.

In a more optimistic frame of mind, Libby took special pains with dinner that night. Perhaps the smell of baked bread and roast lamb would entice her husband to linger over their meal and talk to her. She yearned for that much contact.

Dinner had been ready for a half hour when she started to worry because he hadn't come home yet. A storm had been brewing since late afternoon, and she didn't like the idea of his traveling in a downpour, even if he was being chauffeured.

For want of something to do, she built up the fire, filling the kitchen with warmth. When the phone rang, she had the receiver to her ear on the second ring.

"Yes?" she asked tensely.

"Libby? Are you all right?"

Hearing Vance's voice lightened her mood immediately. "Yes, of course. What about you?"

"I had one of the men drive me to the mine this afternoon. Unfortunately, the rain up here is making the roads impassable at the moment. I'm afraid we'll be stuck here most of the night."

Libby swallowed her disappointment. "I see."

There was a deep silence. "I didn't mean to leave you alone overnight." He sounded genuinely concerned.

"Of course not."

"If you're nervous, phone James."

"I'm fine, really." She paused. "Please, take care of yourself, and hurry home."

"Libby, if we can't make it back until tomorrow, then don't expect me till evening. Charles's plane is due to arrive at six. I'll bring him back to the farm with me."

Her hand tightened on the receiver. Until he said that, she hadn't realized how much she'd counted on being alone with him. Much as she enjoyed Charles's company, the time spent with Vance was precious. She didn't want to share him with anyone else. Which, she told herself grimly, went to show how selfish she'd become. Vance needed Charles, had been anxiously awaiting his arrival.

"Libby?"

"I—I have his room ready," she offered hastily. "I'll plan a prime-rib dinner."

"Charles isn't fussy, so don't knock yourself out. I have to hang up now. Good night, Libby."

"Good night," she said in a husky voice. The line went dead and she slowly replaced the receiver. Tomorrow seemed light-years away; she already missed him terribly. It didn't matter that they hadn't made love. He was so much a part of her, she dreaded the thought of an evening, let alone a lifetime, without him.

WHEN A LAND ROVER with the words Anson Mining on the door pulled up in the driveway at dusk the following evening, Libby fairly raced outside. Her hungry eyes took swift inventory of her husband.

Vance was normally impeccably groomed, but to-night his safari shirt looked rumpled and stained. A full day's growth of beard darkened his jaw. She could tell he'd gone without sleep. Purple shadows under-lined his eyes, which lacked their usual luster. His condition made her wonder just how precarious his situation had been last night. In fact, she was curious to know why he'd gone up to the mine at all. Return-ing to the scene of the accident must have been a grim experience. Libby rubbed the sides of her hips with damp palms, to deter herself from wrapping her arms around him.

"Elizabeth, you grow more beautiful every time I see you."

Her gaze darted to Charles, who sat at the wheel of the Land Rover. He climbed down and gave her a warm kiss on her flushed cheek. "Vance is a lucky devil, you know that?"

She smiled at Charles, trying to ignore the pain that settled around her heart as Vance turned abruptly away at Charles's remark and began to feel his way to the rear of the car.

"He complained of a headache when he picked me up," Charles said in a low voice meant only for her. She nodded, her eyes still on Vance.

"He looks dreadful," she whispered, then in a louder voice, "He's lucky to have you representing him, Charles. I'm thankful you've come."

The famous barrister had distinctive iron-gray hair and a mustache. Though not as tall as Vance, he pos-sessed a powerful build and strong, imposing fea-tures. His intelligent gray eyes didn't miss a detail. He'd recently celebrated his fiftieth birthday but moved like a man ten years younger. Libby suspected he would make a formidable adversary. Apparently Vance thought so, too.

As if on cue, she and Charles both watched Vance as he pulled Charles's cases from the back and made his way to the front door of the farmhouse. She felt a squeeze at her waist. "He's quite a man. Give him time and he'll even be a husband to you one day."

In a few sentences, Charles lifted a weight from her heart and won her affection all in the same process. He understood that her marriage to Vance was not normal, and the reasons for it. She gripped his hand. "He needs you, Charles."

The older man nodded. "He does, indeed." With a hand at the back of her waist, he ushered her into the house. "Your cooperation is of paramount importance at this stage of the game. Can I count on you?" He turned his piercing gaze on her, reminding her of Vance in a lot of ways. Both men were born to be in charge.

"If it came to that, I'd give my life for Vance."

His gray brows furrowed. "Let's pray it doesn't, but I trust Vance has warned you of the dangers."

"Yes."

He pursed his lips. "Good."

Libby escorted him into the living room. He sat down in one of the wing-back bamboo chairs she'd brought in from the *stoep* the day before, along with a matching coffee table. Libby offered him a brandy, since Vance had disappeared. She imagined he'd gone to the bathroom for a shower and shave; she would suggest putting tags on his clothes sometime later, when they were alone.

Libby handed Charles his drink, then sat down, facing her guest. "I knew we'd see you again soon, but

I never imagined it would be under these circumstances.''

Charles stroked his mustache. "You know what they say about life. It's what happens to you when you had other plans.''

A sad smile broke the corners of her pliant mouth. "That's so true, it hurts.'' She lowered her head. "When I flew down here to be with Vance, I had no idea it would cause him more problems.''

"On the contrary, my dear, I'm convinced that your presence will work to our advantage,'' he said kindly.

She brushed a lock of hair from her face. "You really mean that?''

"Love is a miracle in itself. Someplace deep in his psyche, Vance feels the power of your love and it's changing his world, making him stronger than he knows.''

A fine mist covered her eyes. "Thank you for saying that, Charles.''

"Am I interrupting something private?''

Libby turned in her seat, surprised she hadn't heard Vance enter the room. He'd showered and changed into jeans and a black shirt, looking darkly attractive, yet unapproachable. His bronzed face still seemed to be shadowed with pain or fatigue; she had the distinct impression he was ill.

"I brought in the porch furniture, Vance. Take a few more steps and there's a wing-back chair waiting for you. Do you want sherry or brandy?''

"Neither one.''

Libby exchanged a brief glance with Charles. "Why don't the two of you relax while I check on dinner? We'll be eating all our meals in the kitchen for the time being.''

"Vance, my boy, I was telling Elizabeth that if I were twenty years younger, I'd have snapped her up myself."

Vance didn't respond. Libby quickly stood up and headed toward the kitchen. Even for Vance, this mood was too somber. She couldn't shake off the feeling that something was wrong. Was his headache worse? She wondered fearfully if their fall from the horse on Sunday had anything to do with it.

As soon as the gravy was made, she called the men to dinner. Vance found his chair with little difficulty, and Charles followed suit, eyeing the table appreciatively.

"Beautiful, intelligent, *and* domestic," he bantered, winking at her. "You may not be able to see what you're missing, my boy, but you know you got the best, don't you?"

Libby could see that Charles's taunt had gone home. Her husband sat back in the chair with his long legs stretched out in front of him in an attitude of apparent relaxation, but his hand gripped the ice-water tumbler too tightly. She feared it would be crushed in his palm.

Halfway through the meal, Charles sighed. "That's the best Yorkshire pudding I've ever eaten. You must give Marion the recipe." Libby watched his glance rest on Vance, who'd been unusually quiet during dinner. "It occurs to me, Vance, that you have the only gold mine of worth living right inside the confines of your own home."

"You do wonders for a woman's morale," Libby broke in as she saw Vance's features tighten. "How does Marion stand to be parted from you for such long periods?"

He laughed. "Believe it or not, she sends me off quite happily. It makes our reunions more delightful."

"You're to be envied." Her voice caught. She got up from the table to replenish their coffee, noting the bleak expression in Vance's eyes. When she refilled his cup, she took great pains not to touch him.

"Do you want to go back to the living room for a liqueur, Charles?"

He smiled up at Libby, hands folded over his middle. "If you don't mind, I'd prefer to stay right where I am. I don't think I can move."

"I'll take that as a compliment." She sat down once more.

"How much do you know about the accident at the mine, Elizabeth?"

Libby looked first at Charles, then Vance. "Nothing, except that two men were killed."

Charles leaned his elbows on the table. "Vance, it's time she knew all the facts—for a variety of reasons."

"You're right," Vance said after a slight hesitation. He pushed his plate away from him. "The board of inquiry sent their experts to sift through the debris in the tunnel where the cave-in occurred. But they couldn't find even one piece of timber to substantiate my claim that support beams had been used. When we use the stress-pull method, support beams have to be set in place."

Libby frowned. "Don't the blueprints prove that you drew those in?"

Vance rubbed the side of his jaw with his hand. "The blueprints aren't the problem, Libby. It's the engineer's responsibility to make sure the foreman follows the blueprints to the letter. In this case, Peter

Fromms went over everything with Gareth before the charges were set. Peter swears he walked through the entire process several times with Gareth. Gareth insists the support beams were installed. Yet no timbers were found at the scene of the accident.''

"Then someone told a deliberate lie or—"

"Someone removed the timbers before detonation," Vance supplied the rest. "And my investigation yesterday proved the latter beyond any doubt."

"Then it's definitely a murder case."

"That's right," Charles interjected. "But whatever happened—whoever the guilty party is—the ultimate responsibility rests on Vance's shoulders until criminal charges are filed."

"It's so unfair," she cried out in a pained voice.

"You're right." Charles sat forward and placed his palms flat on the table. "You know the essential facts. Now, I'm going to enlist your help."

Her eyes fastened on his. "You know I'd do anything to clear Vance's name."

"Good. I want you to throw a party. And I mean a fabulous party. Pull out all the stops. Drinks, food, music—the works. It's to be a reception celebrating your recent marriage.

"To all those invited, you two will appear so much in love, no one will suspect that you're embroiled in a life-and-death situation. Or that you even harbor any suspicions. Let the champagne flow. Vance can afford it." He grinned as if he were truly enjoying himself.

"While the two of you greet your guests and whisper sweet nothings to each other, I'll circulate among the crowd. No one will know anything about me, except that I was invited to the reception. You'd be surprised what I can pick up when people are unaware. Alcohol has a marvelous way of loosening the tongue.''

Libby looked at her husband. She could imagine what must be running through his mind. ''When should we have this party?''

''The sooner the better. Your list of guests should include everyone from the men working the mines to the hierarchy of the company. To be safe, invite outside friends, government officials, social acquaintances. Make it an affair where people can drop in at their convenience. Keep it informal.''

Vance's expression was anything but pleased as he got to his feet. ''I don't like exposing Libby this way, Charles.''

His concern for her welfare so warmed Libby that she longed to throw herself into his arms, right then and there.

''Neither do I, but it's a perfect opportunity. Everyone who had anything to do with sabotaging the mine will be thrown off base. They won't be expecting a man whose career hangs in the balance—a man who's recently lost his sight—to behave like an ecstatic young bridegroom.''

Vance ran his hands through his hair. ''I don't know.''

''I do,'' Libby asserted. ''What could possibly happen in our own home, Vance? If we're with each other every minute of the time, then there shouldn't be a problem.''

Charles leveled a grateful glance at Libby. ''Elizabeth's right. A party is not exactly an ideal spot to cause trouble, not with so many witnesses. Besides, this whole setup smacks of an amateurish mentality. I don't believe we're dealing with a brilliant criminal mind. It's more likely a person harboring jealousy or out for revenge. A power struggle of some sort. I want to observe this person—or persons—while his guard is down. A wedding party this soon after the tragedy should cause the culprit no end of frustration and possibly force him to reveal it in some way. I'll be watching for that reaction, and for conflicting stories."

Vance's hands dropped to his hips. "So be it. I think we could plan the party for Tuesday or Wednesday of next week. Libby, there's an excellent catering service I've used on several occasions for office parties. They can help you put a celebration of this size together. I'll start phoning people to spread the word."

THE NEXT FEW DAYS passed in a kind of blur for Libby. Once the invitations were extended, Charles and Vance closeted themselves in the library, going over the files and work histories of all Vance's employees, verifying documents, past employment records and possible police records. Many of the foremen and junior engineers had come from other countries before they joined Anson Mining. Vance and Charles worked far into the night while Libby busied herself with preparations for the wedding celebration.

Staff from the hotel catering service arrived in vans on Tuesday, the day before the party, bringing tables, chairs and everything required for the reception. Libby fashioned centerpieces for the tables, which were arranged on the grass in front of the house, and went over the menu with the head chef. She decided to plan everything around an outdoor barbecue. Cases of champagne arrived along with a four-tiered wedding cake to add a touch of authenticity. By four o'clock the next day, the farmhouse and grounds had been transformed.

Libby dressed with great care, although it was only moments before their first guest would arrive. She wanted Vance to be proud of her. From the beginning, he'd confessed that he preferred her black hair loose and flowing—his own bewitching gypsy. She wore it down and brushed it smooth and slipped into the dress she'd bought for the family celebration they'd originally planned in London. It was a knee-length chiffon in pale lavender with a draped bodice and filmy sleeves that buttoned at the wrist. She wore the amethyst earrings Vance had given her for a wedding present, to match her engagement ring. Last, but not least, she pinned the corsage of gardenias to her dress at the shoulder. The flowers were a gift from Charles and the card read, ''Good luck. May the best wife win.''

Libby went in search of Charles to thank him, but stopped in her tracks as she saw Vance emerge from the other bedroom. It was the room she'd envisioned as a nursery that first day; he'd moved in there as soon as the workmen were finished.

He wore a new suit, a light brown silk blend. Brown was his best color, she'd always thought, because it brought out his beautiful velvet eyes. The white shirt and paisley tie set off his mahogany tan. His dark hair, still damp from the shower, curled in tiny tendrils over his forehead and behind his ears.

A fierce desire pierced Libby. He'd always been physically perfect to her, but this afternoon the longing to be held in his arms and kissed into oblivion caused her actual physical pain. A moan escaped her throat, unbidden.

His head lifted. "Libby?"

"How did you know?"

"I can smell the perfume from your gardenias. Since they don't grow on the farm, I assume someone sent them to you." His rigid stance told her he was not pleased.

"Charles gave them to me for luck."

His brows slanted. "The prerogative of the bridegroom, I believe. But recognizing that this bridegroom is derelict in his duties, Charles came to the rescue."

"I'm wearing your wedding present, Vance. The earrings. They're perfect with my dress. But if the corsage offends you, I'll take it off."

He flashed her a sardonic look. "I didn't say the flowers offended me. Quite the contrary. They're the perfect touch for this elaborate farce. Come closer, Libby."

Incredibly, a dart of fear flicked through her. He looked tall and dangerous in a way she'd never seen him before. With a trembling body, she approached him. "What is it?"

Bronzed hands were raised to her neck and encircled it. As if in a trance, Libby stood motionless as he traced a finger along her delicate collarbone to her shoulder. "You smell divine, like a bride should. Do you feel like one, Libby?" His mouth curved into a cruel line. He seemed intent on punishing her—and himself—in some way. "Shall we find out how madly in love you are with your blind man—your sightless lover—your husband who couldn't fight his way out

of a paper bag, let alone defend you from some unseen menace?"

"Stop it, Vance!" she begged, trying to catch her
breath.

Ever so slightly, his hands increased their pressure
on her slender neck. "It's a hideous reality, isn't it,
Libby? And yet, we have to convince everyone out
there that we can't keep our hands off each other.
Convince me, Mrs. Anson." His dark head blocked
out the light as his mouth found hers in a bruising kiss.
His strength would have overpowered any resistance
she might have made, but she didn't fight him. She'd
wanted Vance for so long she welcomed his embrace,
even an embrace born of bitterness. He crushed her
against his hard body and ravished her tender mouth,
allowing no breath, no respite. When it finally got
through to him that she welcomed the savagery of his
lovemaking, he shoved her away, his breath ragged.

"What a consummate little actress you are. Shall we
find Charles and tell him we're ready to greet our
guests?" His eyes glittered as he reached for her hand
and held it almost painfully tight. "Beauty and the
beast!" he quipped on a cruel laugh. He marched
ahead of her, pulling her behind him like a fractious
child. The miracle was that he seemed to know exactly where to go. Libby almost ran to keep up with
him, and all the while her heart was on the verge of
breaking.

"Stay close to me all evening, Libby," he warned as
they entered the foyer. "If anyone arouses your suspicions in the slightest, let me know. I'll just be
thankful when this is over."

By eight in the evening, Libby had met more than
three hundred invited guests. Anson Mining em-

ployed a miniature city. It staggered her to realize that Vance headed everything—that he'd founded his own company and built it to be so successful. Her admiration for his brilliance and business acumen increased in quantum leaps as she was introduced to guest after guest. Everyone seemed to hold him in the highest regard. A fierce pride in her husband caused a permanent smile to radiate from Libby's face as Vance guided her among the throng. She could scarcely believe that anyone from this group would wish him harm.

All the guests began to gather together. Someone proposed a toast to the happy couple. Everyone hailed and cheered them. The warm welcome was so genuine and affectionate, Libby thought she detected a fine mist covering Vance's dark eyes from time to time. When the initial din subsided, Vance put a possessive hand on Libby's shoulder. She could feel its warmth through the thin fabric of her dress.

"So you won't all be consumed by curiosity," Vance joked, "I'll announce here and now, and this is official, that we've weathered the storm...and business will proceed as usual." He would have gone on, but everyone applauded and he was forced to wait a few minutes. "As you know by now, I didn't let any grass grow under my feet the last time I went to England. While I was there, I entered into a brand new partnership."

His hand slid to Libby's slender waist in an intimate gesture. "Meet my beautiful wife, Libby, who has managed to make me the happiest man on earth."

He ran his fingers through her glossy black hair before pressing a kiss to the side of her neck. The spontaneous clapping and whistles at his display of possessiveness sent a hot flush over her body that people couldn't fail to detect. Hectic color filled her cheeks. "Speech! Speech!"

"When I returned to England for a vacation a few years ago, I discovered a new family living on the property next to my father's. He invited them for cocktails. I was prepared to indulge him for a short while and leave. But Libby walked into the drawing room. She took away my breath then, and I haven't caught it since."

Libby clung to Vance, amazed by what he said because it had happened the same way for her. There'd never been anyone but Vance from the first moment she laid eyes on him.

The usual comments about newlyweds came one after the other. Vance squeezed her again and planted a firm, lingering kiss on her parted mouth. After what had gone on between them in the hall, before the party, his loving behavior in front of everyone came as a shock. Knowing the reason for his pretense robbed her of the ecstasy the moment should have held.

Though Vance warned everybody against talking business, he was soon besieged with questions on policies, technical data and personnel problems that only he could answer. The boss was back now, and everyone seemed relieved. His blindness in no way affected his authority or expertise; Libby had always known that, and if Vance entertained any doubts, they were being put to rest for good. All he had to do was step into the room and he was automatically in command. Anson Mining was where he belonged.

As Libby watched him getting caught up in the jargon of his business dealings—even while the partying continued—she became convinced that their reception had begun to heal some of her husband's wounds. He was a leader, back in gear, already discussing new projects, making new plans. One would never guess that he had a sword hanging over his head—or that he'd lost his sight. Even if Vance wouldn't let her be a real wife to him, she'd always remember this hour with joy.

The crowd started to thin around eleven, but Libby saw no sign of Charles. He stayed out on the *stoep* near the bar, ready to pounce on any clue that might come his way.

"Vance? The caterer is giving me the sign. I need to bring out more champagne," she whispered. "Stay here and I'll be right back."

"I'll give you exactly two minutes," he whispered into her silky hair, sending delightful shivers through her body. Reluctantly, she broke free of his arm, which had been around her shoulders, and headed for the back porch, leaving him to a lively discussion with one of his junior engineers. Their stock of champagne had dwindled. She pulled the three remaining bottles from the box and hurried into the dining room to put them on ice.

"Mrs. Anson," an unfamiliar voice called from behind her. Libby turned around. "You probably don't remember me."

She gazed at the auburn-haired man whose tan was almost as dark as her husband's. "You're Peter Fromms, aren't you?"

He gave her an engaging and slightly lopsided grin. "You *do* remember. The last time we met, you couldn't take your eyes off your husband, either."

"Am I that obvious?" she asked smiling.

"Afraid so. As I recall, we were introduced in the swimming pool, but you were watching Vance play water polo and I got the distinct impression your mind was elsewhere."

"It probably was, but I enjoyed talking with your wife, Nancy. Where is she?"

Sadness filled his eyes for an instant. "She's in Perth with her family. We're separated at the moment."

"I didn't realize."

He stared at her as if weighing her words. "Why should you? Besides, this is your night. Will you dance with me, or do you think your husband might object?"

The old Vance wouldn't mind, she mused to herself. The new Vance was unpredictable. And she had the strangest feeling that Peter Fromms was treading very carefully. Why? He and Vance had been such close friends at one time.

"Forget I asked the question," he said, not unkindly.

"Please don't think me rude, but I promised Vance I wouldn't be long. Why don't we dance our way over to him?"

He hid his surprise well as he led her into the center of the room where a half-dozen other couples were dancing. "You're more beautiful than ever," he said on a sober note. "Vance keeps pictures of you on his desk at the office. What a tragedy that he can't see you anymore."

Coming from someone else, the remark might have seemed offensive to Libby. Although she couldn't have explained why, she sensed a heartfelt sincerity, a genuine display of emotion behind Peter's words.

"But it's not the end of the world," she told him gently. "Vance and I share something much deeper than the physical."

"If you don't mind, Fromms, my wife and I are going to get a little physical right now. Aren't we, darling?" Libby almost gasped at the restrained anger in Vance's tone and the unexpected harshness of his touch. Again she wondered why there was so much tension between the two men. And what, if anything, did it have to do with her?

CHAPTER SEVEN

PETER DIPPED HIS HEAD in a silent salute as Vance whisked Libby away with the ease of a sighted man. Libby clung to Vance as they danced in place to the music.

"Was Peter coming on to you?"

She stopped dancing and looked up at him in surprise. "No. Anything but."

Vance frowned. "He usually gets out of line when he's had a few drinks. If he thought he could get away with it, he'd make a serious pass at you."

She blinked. "You must have him mixed up with someone else. As far as I could tell, he hadn't had a drink."

"That's surprising." He stroked her wrist with his thumb, perhaps unaware of his actions. But the merest touch set Libby's pulse racing. "Any passable female—even a married one like Marj Dean—is fair game. He's not to be trusted."

"I don't understand. He was a good friend of yours. He and Nancy even visited your home in England. Has something happened between the two of you?"

"You'll have to ask Nancy. She left him."

"Vance, that doesn't sound like you. They're both very nice people."

"I know she liked you. That's why she asked you to go shopping with her in London that time—to get you away from Peter's irresistible charms."

"What?" Libby couldn't believe what she was hearing.

"He paid you an inordinate amount of attention the night the two of you were introduced."

For some reason, Vance wouldn't let it alone. "You're exaggerating. If he'd bothered me, I would have remembered. I know a real pass when I see one coming."

His mouth hardened. "With your kind of beauty, I can imagine."

"Vance, what's this all about?"

"Just take my word for it. Peter was on the prowl that night. You were—always have been—a desirable woman. But you weren't available. The fact that you didn't respond to him must have been a blow to his pride."

Libby had no idea Vance had been harboring all this jealousy. "Why do you still employ him if that's how you feel?"

He resumed dancing with her. "That's a good question. Probably because he was my best friend once, and because he's a brilliant engineer. He could head his own company. At one time, I thought we might go into partnership together.

"But his drinking binges are common knowledge. When Nancy left him, he wanted another chance. I had to put him on probation for several months. Still—"

"Still what?" Libby pulled far enough away to look up at her husband. His face had gone an ashen color and perspiration broke out on his brow and upper lip. "Vance? What's wrong?"

He leaned heavily against her. "Don't let on to anyone, Libby. Keep dancing over to the door. It's a headache, that's all."

"Like the one you had the night you brought Charles home to dinner?" she asked anxiously. She was supporting his weight to some degree as they moved toward the bedroom. No one seemed to notice them go inside or see her lock the door. And any people who did would probably just assume they wanted a moment's privacy. "Lie down. I'm going to call Dr. Stillman."

"What in heaven's name for?" He stretched out on the bed, covering his eyes with his arm. "I get headaches on occasion."

"Only since your fall the day we went riding. You were supposed to visit Dr. Stillman last week. I've been worried ever since."

"Let's get something straight. I'll decide when and if I need to see a doctor. Go back to the party and stay with Charles. Explain to him. But if anyone else asks, say I'll be out in a few minutes. Don't say anything about the headache."

"I'll cooperate if you will." She went to the bathroom for water and two of his prescribed tablets. "Here." She waited until he took them. He looked ill. "Please don't get up again, Vance. People are starting to go home."

"We'll see." His voice sounded strained.

"I promise to hurry."

A group of men in the higher echelons of the company intercepted her as she made her way to the *stoep*, thanking her for the party. Several said they wanted to say good-night to Vance.

"He'll be out in a few minutes," she said, hoping they'd take no notice. Charles, who was part of this small crowd, approached her.

"Tell Vance I'll see him soon. I'm going back to Martin's place. He's invited a bunch of us over for a drink."

"That's right," Martin Dean agreed. "I promised Marj I wouldn't be out too late. She's been feeling poorly for the past few days."

Libby shook his hand. "Come again soon, Martin. And bring Marj. I'm sorry she hasn't been well. Maybe we can get together for dinner one night next week."

"She'd love that. Tell Vance I'll talk to him in the morning. It's important," he muttered in a low voice so only she could hear, his eyes focused on Peter Fromms, who stood several yards away talking to one of the engineers. First Vance, now Martin. Under the circumstances, Libby couldn't understand why Peter was still on the payroll.

"I'll tell him. Good night."

Several hands lifted in farewell as the crowd disappeared out the front door. For the next half hour, Libby mingled with the last of the guests. If anyone asked about Vance, she explained that he was needed somewhere else. Peter seemed to have gone.

Because the evening had been so emotionally draining, Libby felt more exhausted than usual once all the guests had left. The catering staff didn't take long to put things in order and then they left, too. Finally, well after midnight, she and Vance were alone. It felt wonderful.

She slipped off her heels and tiptoed to Vance's room. The light was still on. She saw that he had taken off his suit and was sound asleep, his arm covering his eyes. She listened closely, but his breathing sounded normal to her. She hoped he'd sleep off his headache. She couldn't bear to think of him in any more pain.

Once in her own room, Libby pulled off her dress. A few minutes later, she climbed in between the sheets of the double bed. But sleep didn't come for a long time, despite the fact that her body felt like a dead-weight. Her thoughts went from Peter to Vance and back again. As for the guests who'd come to their home tonight, she couldn't fathom that any of them had the mentality to kill or to destroy a man's career—a man who'd given them jobs and security. Inevitably, her thoughts strayed back to Vance. He'd behaved like the adoring bridegroom tonight; his performance had fooled everyone. She turned on her stomach and stifled her sobs in the pillow.

Libby awakened late in the morning. When she peeked into Vance's room, she discovered that his bed had already been made. James's work, no doubt. It hurt Libby that Vance had turned to his farm manager—and not to her—for help with personal tasks. But James came and went so quietly, she was scarcely aware of his presence. Disappointed not to talk to Vance, she padded barefoot into the kitchen for a glass of juice and found his note. James had driven him to Nairobi. If she needed him, she could try the flat. He thanked Libby for the wonderful party and assured her that he'd repay her at some future date. The note was written in his own bold hand, but it slanted across the page like a child's, in uneven lines.

Libby reread the note before crushing it between her hands and tossing it in the wastebasket. Needing to channel the hurt into something physical, she cleaned the farmhouse from one end to the other and wore herself out in the process.

Later in the day, she called both sets of parents to tell them about the reception. She was careful to avoid mentioning Vance's company problems. It could only worry them more.

Vance and Charles arrived back at the farm around eight. One look at her husband and Libby knew something was wrong. "You go ahead and eat without me." He flung the words at her the minute he felt his way into the front hall. Her heart lurched. He had no word of greeting for her. Nothing.

"You look like death, Vance. I know your headaches have been growing worse."

He paused in the doorway to the living room. "It came on during the drive. I'll take some pills. It'll pass. Then I'll join you." She was shocked at how strained his voice sounded, as though every sentence required a fresh burst of effort.

Charles flicked Libby a speaking glance as she offered him a glass of wine. "We've been at the flat most of the day, talking. He had two bad spells while I was there."

Libby's voice shook. "His headaches are so terrible, I'm afraid one day he'll just collapse."

"What did the doctor say when Vance was released from the hospital?"

She ran a slender hand through her hair. "He said a certain amount of pain was normal, but I don't think there's anything normal about these spells.

"I might as well tell you. A few weeks ago he fell while we were out riding." She quickly related the details. "Vance refuses to see Dr. Stillman. Maybe you can influence him to see the doctor tomorrow for a checkup. He won't listen to me."

Charles pushed his fingertips together. "Your husband has a mind of his own, but then I'm not telling you anything you don't know." He smiled in compassion. "I'll see what I can do."

He got to his feet. "Perhaps we could have a light dinner and then let's call it a night. I didn't get to bed till after three. Tomorrow morning we'll all be rested and I'll fill you in on what I've discovered so far."

Libby felt relief that Charles wanted to bring the evening to an end. She couldn't concentrate on anything knowing Vance was suffering so much pain. Not only that, but something bothered her. Something shadowy hovering in the recesses of her mind. She couldn't put her finger on it, but it was there. Something she'd noticed last night. On impulse, Libby went back to Vance's room and stepped inside the doorway. All she could hear was the slow, even sound of his breathing. Light from the hallway revealed that he lay on his back again, more or less sprawled out on the bed in an attitude of relaxation.

Why she flipped on the light switch, she didn't stop to analyze, but when she did, the reaction of the previous night occurred. His arm went to his face—*as if to shield his eyes from the light!*

Goose bumps sprang up on the back of her neck until her skin crawled. She turned off the light, and his arm fell to his side again. She covered her mouth to smother the gasp that rose to her throat. Without wasting another moment, she hurried to Charles's room and knocked on the door. He answered quickly, still dressed in his suit. She put a finger to his lips.

"Come with me," she whispered. "I want you to do something for me. I'll explain later. Just trust me. Don't make a sound."

"All right." He followed her to the next room. Vance still lay in the same position, on his back. Charles glanced at him and then at Libby with questioning eyes.

"Watch what happens when I turn on the light," she whispered, and flipped the switch. This time it took three seconds before his arm again moved to his eyes. As far as Libby was concerned, the evidence was conclusive. Her eyes locked with Charles's. "That has happened every time I've turned on the light. Now, watch!" She turned off the light and within seconds, his arm slipped down to the sheet.

Charles looked dumbstruck. He reached for the switch and flicked it on. Vance groaned, and turned over in the bed to bury his face in the pillow. Charles gripped Libby's upper arm. Streams of unspoken words flowed between them. When he turned off the light, a soft sigh came from Vance. Charles guided Libby out of the room and down the hall to the library.

"You must call his doctor immediately."

"I'm going to," Libby asserted, leafing rapidly through a small leather-bound address book.

"If I hadn't witnessed it with my own eyes, I don't think I would have believed you." His voice cracked with emotion.

Libby's hand shook as she dialed the doctor's home phone number. He answered on the third ring.

"Dr. Stillman here."

"Doctor? It's Libby Anson. Something has happened you need to know about." In a torrent of words, Libby related everything. Charles sat on the edge of the desk, listening.

"I want to see him in my office first thing in the morning. It's absolutely essential. But under no circumstances do I want you to tell him what you've discovered. It might mean something. Then again, it could be insignificant." His words dashed Libby's hopes. "Has he been bothered by headaches?"

"Yes. And the pain seems to be getting progressively worse. I can't go on pretending this isn't serious."

"I agree. Do whatever it takes, but have your husband at the hospital tomorrow morning."

"I will. I promise." They said goodbye, and she replaced the receiver. She looked over at Charles with an encouraged smile, but it faded as she saw Vance hovering in the doorway.

"To whom were you making such a solemn promise, Libby?"

All the color drained from Libby's face. Charles stood up abruptly and reached for her hand. A terrible tension pervaded the room. When Vance interrogated, he didn't leave it alone until he got the answers he wanted.

"Dr. Stillman."

"Indeed?"

"You've been suffering from headaches since that fall. When you didn't want to eat dinner tonight, I got worried and called him. I needed to find out if this is normal. He said it is, but he still wants to see you in his office in the morning, and he won't take no for an answer."

"I urged her to call him, Vance." Charles came to the rescue in his courtroom voice. "I can't do a proper investigation if I have to worry about your physical condition. As you know, the board of inquiry will be taking your deposition on Monday. Their questions will drain you, and I must be absolutely certain that you're fit in body, as well as mind."

Libby squeezed his hand in gratitude. "Concussion is nothing to sneeze at, Vance. To be honest, Dr. Stillman sounded quite angry that you didn't reschedule the appointment I made with him. He blames me for not making sure you followed through. I won't take the blame again."

"I've had a few headaches," Vance conceded, moving into the room with his hands in his pockets. "Nothing more serious than that." His attitude bordered on hostility.

"Maybe not," Charles said calmly, "but I take your physical well-being seriously, considering you have a deposition coming up."

Vance rubbed his neck. "You've made your point. I'll call for an appointment."

"That's a relief," Charles patted Vance's shoulder with affection. "I'll say good-night and leave you two alone. This weekend, I'd like Elizabeth to hear about the information I amassed at the party. Between the three of us, we ought to be able to sort things out. I have a feeling we're going to turn this case around with a little more time."

"That's good news, Charles," he answered. "But I agree. This can wait until later. I'm afraid my brain ceases to function after hours where business is concerned."

Libby darted an anxious glance at Vance. What he'd just said was an outright lie. He had a brain like a steel trap, any time of the day or night. Libby could tell Vance was far from satisfied with her explanation about the phone call. Did he intend to question her further? He could be relentless when driven past a certain point. Taking Vance's obvious hint, Charles waved good-night to Libby and left the library.

Vance looked larger than life, standing there in the center of the room, so dark and remote. His body was taut, as if he held his emotions in check. She couldn't believe he didn't want to talk about the investigation with Charles. Surely it was the most important issue in his life. The fact that Vance wanted to be alone with her now was not a good sign. He seemed to be stalking her. Why?

"I may be blind," he began quietly, "but I know when something isn't right. What's going on, Libby? I want an answer, even if I have to keep you here all night."

"I don't know what you're talking about. Charles and I already told you—we were concerned enough for your welfare to call the doctor. That's all."

"No." He shook his head, and flashed her that wintry smile. "You might be able to fool everyone else, but I'm Vance, remember? I know every mood and facet of your personality. You're hiding something from me."

"Don't be ridiculous." She backed away from him and stumbled over the wastebasket.

"You're frightened," he said softly. His hands curled into fists in a gesture of utter exasperation. "Charles was covering up for you, wasn't he?"

Libby was stunned. His wild accusation that she and Charles were keeping something from him rendered her speechless, incapable of moving.

"I'm right, aren't I?" He took a step toward her, moving with a certain menace. "What's wrong, Libby? I have a right to know! Why did you call the doctor? I heard you tell him the pain was worse. Whose pain? Yours?"

"Mine?"

"You hurt yourself when we fell, didn't you? Now you're trying to pretend, but it won't work. Where did you injure yourself? Tell me!" he demanded, firing one question after the other. When she realized all this emotion was due to his fear for her health, her anxiety fled. She took a deep, shuddering breath that her secret was still safe.

"I'm fine, Vance."

"I don't believe you."

"Then I'll have to convince you." She covered the distance between them and put her arms around his neck as she used to. "Feel for yourself," she whispered, melting against him. A tremor passed through his body, but he held himself rigid. "I've never felt better in my life." She pressed lingering kisses along his taut jaw and ran her hands over his upper arms and broad shoulders. Out of a need she could no longer suppress, she rose up on tiptoe to brush his mouth with her lips. The concern he'd shown bordered on panic, and it proved to her how much he did care.

He gave a low groan, as his hands moved possessively over her slender shoulders and down her back. With an urgency that communicated his hunger, he crushed her to him, and they fused together like two halves of a whole. "Are you satisfied that I'm all right?" she whispered.

"No," he answered in a husky voice, nuzzling her tender throat with his lips. "Not until I've loved you completely." A languor stole over Libby as he lifted her in his strong arms with effortless grace and started for her bedroom. Instinct must have told him where to go, since at this point Libby had lost all awareness of her surroundings. Closing the door behind him, he placed her gently on the bed and settled next to her.

"Come here to me, sweetheart," he urged, drawing her closer still. "I want to love you all night." His hands were smoothing and stroking her long, black hair. Her breath came in small gasps when he kissed the hollows in her cheeks and at her throat. "I've needed to feel you like this for so long. Years..." His deep voice trembled with emotion.

"Vance," she cried softly, cupping his face in her hands and kissing his eyes. In a surge of longing, she pulled his dark head close and buried her face in his hair. "Love me... love me."

"I don't think you need to ask me that," he murmured against her lips. In a sinuous movement, his hand slid beneath her hair to her nape as he sought her mouth with his own. "Your skin is like satin. I can feel your heart beating and hear your breath catch with the slightest movement of my hand.

"How many nights have I imagined you like this in my arms, willing me to love you? I need to love all of you until there's no part that doesn't belong to me." His mouth began working its magic.

Every kiss, every caress awakened Libby, elevating her to a new level of rapture. She delighted in the feel of his skin against hers, his mouth like sweet wine.

When she touched him, every muscle and sinew responded to her melting warmth. The night began as a series of revelations, each more wonderful than the last, until their cries mingled and she clung helplessly to her husband, her lover. Tears of joy trickling from her eyes were savored by his lips as he kissed them away, and then, the whole, sacred, beautiful process began all over again.

"Vance..." she whispered, trying to find the words.

His mouth said them for her, devouring her, and once again she was lost, accepting pleasure and giving it with a newfound freedom that brought ecstasy.

Some time before the dawn, she heard her name on his lips. The longing in his voice stirred her to a breathless excitement. She sought his mouth and felt his hand tighten in her hair. He embraced her with a fierce abandonment her body had been aching for. Afterward, she drifted into a contented sleep, a sleep filled with dreams of the man she loved.

"VANCE?"

When there was no response, Libby reached out for her husband, needing the same fulfillment she'd known over and over again during the night. Her hand felt the coolness of the sheet, and she was suddenly wide-awake. *He'd gone.*

She glanced at her bedside clock. Almost noon. It didn't seem possible she'd slept this late. Her glance took in the pile of clothes still lying in a heap on the floor by the bed. Memories of their passionate night swamped her with love and longing. No amount of rhetoric could begin to describe the incredible joy of belonging to him at last....

She slid from the bed and threw on her bathrobe. A quick tour of the farmhouse verified her fears. Both Vance and Charles had gone to Nairobi in the Land Rover. As far as she was concerned, last night had altered their marriage irrevocably. But she wanted that reassurance from Vance, wanted to hear it from his own lips. If she waited until he came home from work, she'd go mad with her thoughts and feelings.

Throughout the night, Vance had created a time of enchantment for the two of them, when nothing mattered but to love and be loved. Now, Libby had the deep satisfaction of knowing she'd made him happy. But with the morning, everything seemed different. He'd left their bed without a word. She thought she knew what was in his heart, but she needed to know what was going on in his mind, too. That wasn't something they could discuss over the phone. If she surprised him at the office, maybe they could go out to dinner and talk . . . spend the night at a hotel. They had the future to talk about.

Full of the confidence that can only come after a night such as they had shared, Libby was certain he wouldn't mind if she made an appearance. He'd insisted that she stay away until the reception. But now it was over, and she saw no reason to keep out of sight. She wanted to see his corporate offices, feel more a part of his life. If the truth be known, she couldn't wait to be held in his arms again. The night hadn't been long enough.

By midafternoon, Libby was ready. She started the Jeep and headed for Nairobi, the overnight bag beside her, packed with clothes and toiletries for both of them, in the hope that Vance would be amenable to going to a hotel. She'd showered and dressed with care, wearing a new French-blue, raw silk dress. For a change, she caught her hair back in a chignon, wanting to look beautiful for her husband, even if her husband couldn't see her. Her plans for the two of them were decidedly intimate and exciting, and she couldn't get to town fast enough.

Three miles outside the city limits, the temperature pointed to hot. Biting her lip in frustration, Libby slowed to a stop and turned off the motor. The water in the radiator gurgled noisily. She couldn't help wondering if the accident during the rainstorm a few weeks before had anything to do with her present difficulty. She let the Jeep sit for ten minutes, then started it again, pulling into the first service station she could find.

To her consternation, the attendant discovered that the Jeep thermostat needed to be replaced. It might not be fixed until the next day, but she could check back later in the evening.

Under the circumstances, Libby had no choice but to call a taxi to drive her to Vance's office. She brought the overnight bag along, refusing to be discouraged by a minor setback.

Vance's company comprised a conglomerate of departments with plush offices that took up two full floors of space in the new mining complex. After a short ride in the elevator, Libby found herself on the floor reserved for Vance's suite and those of his board of directors. Her first impression of space, glass, chrome and plants paled beside the magnificence of the African art dominating the reception area. One of the secretaries caught sight of Libby as she stepped out of the lift and ushered her into Vance's private suite of rooms immediately. Libby put a detaining hand on her arm.

"Is my husband alone?" she asked quietly.

"Yes, Mrs. Anson."

"Then I'd like to surprise him, if you don't mind."

"Of course not." The secretary smiled and went back to her desk, eyeing Libby with keen interest.

Trying to quell the beating of her heart, Libby slipped inside the room, not making a sound. Vance sat behind a walnut desk in a large swivel chair that happened to be turned so it faced away from the entry.

She put down her things and tiptoed toward him, leaning over to press a kiss against his neck. "I missed you this morning. So much that I couldn't stay away," she whispered, walking around so she could sit on his lap. She stopped in her tracks. The man writhing in agony before her bore little resemblance to the husband who had trembled with desire in her arms last night.

Vance lay back in the leather chair, white-faced. His eyes were closed. She'd seen that look on his face several times in the past week—the look of intense pain. At her slight gasp, his eyes flickered open. He sat up in the chair immediately. His features hardened, and the dark brows furrowed menacingly. "I thought I told you this office was off limits!"

His anger threw her completely. "Since I met everyone on your staff the other night, I don't see the need to stay away." She took a step closer. "How long have you been like this? Anyone can see you're ill. This can't go on, Vance."

"At the risk of repeating myself, my health is my own affair." His taut mouth thinned in distaste. "Your pity sickens me, Libby."

She rocked in place. "Pity?"

"You can stop your playacting now." His boardroom voice held that authoritative ring. "Your sacrifice has been noted. Last night you made a heroic gesture for a blind man, but you needn't fear that I expect a repeat performance. To be blunt, a marriage based on pity isn't what I had in mind."

If he'd slapped her across the room, he couldn't have done more damage. "You call making love with your husband a gesture?" Her voice shook with anguish.

His deadly smile frightened her. "What else would you call it? Do the blind man a favor. Let him pretend for a little while that he has all his faculties," he mocked sarcastically. "I have to admit you're a real actress, Libby. Even now, knowing what you're capable of, there's a part of me that responds to that breathless emotion. Last night..." He paused. "Your performance was astonishing. I thought I'd gone to heaven and taken you there with me."

"Stop it, Vance!"

"If it gives you any satisfaction, I lost my head in your arms. For a little while, I sold my soul. Fortunately, morning came, and with it, sanity."

"How can you say that?" She clutched the rim of one of the chairs like a lifeline.

"How can I not?" he came back mercilessly. "I told you I didn't want you here in the first place, Libby. What happened last night was the result of a long period of deception for my company's benefit. But you've served your purpose. Charles is onto pertinent information, so we can quit the pretense. Our marriage is over. It should never have taken place at all—another bad judgment on my part for which I take full blame and responsibility.''

"And I have nothing to say about it?''

Vance sat forward, placing his palms on the desk. "I'm going to divorce you. Charles will explain the details. I've worked out an appropriate settlement to compensate you for your generosity to me last night. You went beyond the call of duty, Libby, and for that you'll receive a handsome reward.''

"A reward?'' Her cry reverberated in the room. "How can you say that to me? How can you? Well, I won't give you a divorce!'' A light-headed sensation forced Libby to lean against the chair for support.

"I think you will.'' The absolute calm of his voice unnerved her. "I've made a reservation for a flight leaving Nairobi in the morning. By tomorrow night, you'll be back at White Oaks. Pack what you need for now, and I'll see that the rest of your belongings are crated and shipped to England as quickly as possible.''

"And if I should leave Kenya carrying your child, then what?'' she taunted. Neither of them had thought beyond gratifying each other's needs last night.

A pulse throbbed at his temple. "Then I'll set up a trust fund. I don't shirk my responsibilities.''

Something snapped inside Libby. "You'd actually deny yourself the joy of holding your own child in your arms? Of being a father?''

His eyes narrowed. "A blind father, don't forget. At any rate, we're talking in possibilities, not facts. Perhaps now is the time to tell you that I've put the farm on the market. I promised Martin a long time ago that he could have first option to buy, should I decide to sell it. He and Marj are driving out on Sunday to make a detailed inspection before we close the transaction. He's already given me earnest money. That's the reason I want you gone in the morning.''

Libby couldn't fathom it. "The farm is your pride and joy, Vance. You can't give it up. I won't let you! For heaven's sakes, why are you doing this?''

"In case you hadn't noticed, I'm blind. The flat will serve my needs adequately for the rest of my born days. The nearness to my offices makes it a practical arrangement—assuming I still have a company at some later date. To make a long story short, I no longer need you or want you in my life.''

"You talk as if I were an unsatisfactory employee you've fired. You can't get rid of me in quite the same way.''

"I thought I could." His mocking smile infuriated her. "Until you agree to the divorce, I won't give you one penny. And without a home to live in, I don't see that you have a choice, except to leave. Here's your airline ticket." He pulled an envelope out of his top drawer and dropped it on the table. "Charles will be at the farm by seven to drive you to the airport tomorrow and to discuss the divorce with you. I think that's everything.''

"You can tell Charles he's wasting his time." She turned on her heel and started for the door, then whirled around. "I'm not leaving Kenya, Vance. When you come to your senses, you can reach me at the New Stanley Hotel tomorrow." Her voice shook as she walked out of his office with as much dignity as she could manage. Was she also walking out of his life?

CHAPTER EIGHT

"MRS. ANSON?"

Libby turned her head in the direction of a man's voice as she stood in front of the elevator doors. Peter Fromms was standing beside her, but she'd been too distraught to notice. "Are you all right? You're as pale as a ghost."

"I'm hungry." Her wan smile didn't reach her eyes. "I should have eaten lunch before coming into town. It's nice of you to be concerned. How are you?"

The doors opened and they stepped inside. "Do you want the truth?" He expelled a weary sigh. "It's been a rotten day, and it's not over yet."

Libby glanced at her watch. "It's after five."

He tipped his bush hat to the back of his head. "I have to drive out to the Naivasha mine on business."

Libby eyed his work clothes dispassionately. "Are you leaving immediately?"

"Yes." His brows lifted. "Why do you ask?"

"I wonder if I could drive with you as far as the city limits. I had to leave the Jeep at a service station so the thermostat could be replaced. Would you mind? Vance has business for a few more hours and I need to get back home."

If he felt surprise at her request, he covered it beautifully. "Be my guest. However, I must warn you that the company truck leaves a lot to be desired. You'll have to contend with a broken spring, and you're not exactly dressed for roughing it.'' His glance was full of male admiration.

"I'll risk it."

The doors opened onto the main floor. "So be it. If you'll wait here in the lobby, I'll bring the truck around front."

"Thank you, Mr. Fromms."

His mouth widened into a friendly smile. "I hate formality. Couldn't you call me Peter?"

"That works both ways, you know. I'm Libby."

He nodded his pleasure. "I'll be right back."

As Peter started out the doors, Martin Dean ambled in. His glance flicked from Peter to Libby. "I say. This is a lovely surprise, Mrs. Anson. Are you just coming to see Vance?" While he was speaking, Peter disappeared outside.

"Actually, I'm on my way home." She felt disinclined to talk to Martin Dean. She not only disliked the way he ignored Peter, but she wondered what kind of man would be so eager to move into another man's home. If he were her husband's friend, wouldn't he try to persuade Vance to keep the farm, not to give it up?

"By the way, did Vance tell you that Marj and I are coming out on Sunday to take a look around?"

She sucked in her breath. "Yes, he mentioned it."

He laughed nervously, tugging at his earlobe. "We can hardly believe our good fortune because—"

"Excuse me, Mr. Dean," Libby broke in, "but my ride is waiting for me. I'm sorry we can't talk any longer."

"No problem. It will keep for another time." He responded pleasantly but his manner was cool.

"Goodbye." Libby hurried through the doors to the truck but had the distinct feeling that she was being watched.

Peter started the motor but he didn't head into the traffic. Instead, he turned to her, a slight frown on his face. "I'm not your husband's favorite person, Libby, and I can tell you right now that Martin will inform him that you're driving with me. It doesn't worry me, but I wanted you to know the facts. I'll understand if you change your mind."

"I know more than you think," she said quietly. "He told me you were best friends at one time, that you'd even talked about going into partnership together."

Peter blinked. Finally he said, "Perhaps that was true once, but a lot of water has flowed under the bridge since then. Certain parties have—" He broke off. "Look Libby, by simply driving you to the service station, I'm going to inspire gossip."

Libby had the feeling that Peter had been badly hurt in some way. His hesitation to risk taking her anywhere made her want to know him better and find out what had gone wrong between him and Vance.

"Are you worried about your reputation or mine?"

"Yours, of course. Mine couldn't be worse. To top it off, I'm the prime suspect in the disaster inquest. I'm all but washed up. Your husband won't approve of your being with me, even for a short ride in a company truck."

Libby settled herself more comfortably on the seat, suddenly remembering she'd left her overnight case in Vance's office. "I'm not going to pretend I don't know what you're talking about, but Vance still has you working for the company. That has to mean something." She paused, then added, "He told me things haven't gone too well for you."

"That's a surprise." Watching for an opening in the late-afternoon traffic, he swung the truck into the lane. "Did I mention that Nancy left me?"

"Yes. I'm sorry your marriage didn't work out."

His hands tightened their grip on the steering wheel. "Thanks. I'm sorry, too, although I've never admitted that to anyone before."

Strangely enough, Libby believed him. "Would you answer me something in complete honesty?"

"Would you believe me?"

"Yes," Libby replied with conviction. "Vance says you made a pass at me that time you came to London with Nancy. Did you?"

He gave a short laugh. "Oh, yes. Indeed I did."

Libby was astonished at his frankness. "Why don't I remember? You couldn't have done anything offensive."

"You didn't know I existed. You were totally absorbed in Vance."

"Peter... why did you do it?"

"Vance and I go back a long way together. I used to wonder why he never married and settled down, or at least lived with someone. He had ample opportunity, believe me." Libby could imagine. "That night in London, I caught him looking at you by the pool. I'd never seen him look at another woman like that. I did a stupid thing. I decided to pay attention to you to see how he'd respond... to test my theory. I told Nancy what I intended to do and she egged me on because she was curious, too. Unfortunately, the whole thing backfired. I never thought Vance could be that deeply affected by anything or anyone."

Libby sat spellbound. "I had absolutely no idea."

"Vance was civil enough after that, but he never forgave me and never let me explain. Looking back on it now, I must have been out of my mind. It was an incredibly immature thing to do."

In one sense, it thrilled Libby that as long as three years ago, Vance had such strong feelings for her. On the other hand, she could easily imagine how hurt Peter must have been when Vance shut him out. Remembering the scene in Vance's office, her eyes closed in pain. *What was she going to do?*

"Nancy asked you to go shopping with her, hoping to find out if you'd been offended, too," he continued, unaware of her chaotic emotions. "We wanted to make it up to both of you." He rubbed his jaw. "The thing is, Nancy and I considered Vance our dearest friend. We were delighted that he had a secret love. But what started out in good fun ended in disaster. Overnight our friendship disintegrated. Like the cave-in, everything fell down around my head. Is that enough honesty for you?"

Libby stared at him. "I knew there had to be an explanation. When it's the right time, I'll tell Vance the truth."

A low laugh rumbled out of him and with it, a hint of remorse. "He'll never listen, particularly with *you* championing my cause."

"Peter, I've never known Vance to invite anyone else from Kenya to his home in England. He obviously cared for you and Nancy a great deal to extend that kind of hospitality."

"Don't you see?" he groaned. "Flirting with you was like a slap in the face. I abused his trust."

"But he should have let you explain," Libby argued. "And if I hadn't been so blind, I could have picked up on the situation before it grew any worse. Peter, please remember that he hasn't given up on your friendship completely or he'd never have kept you with the company."

"He's regretting it now. Martin has his ear these days. He warned Vance that I—" He paused. "I'm talking too much. Now where is this service station?"

Libby gave him directions. She wasn't surprised to learn that the repairs to the Jeep weren't completed yet. It might be another hour before she could drive back to the farm.

"I'm not leaving you here alone," Peter insisted, shaking his head. "Since you admit you're hungry, and I need a meal sometime this evening, let's drive to a hotel and have dinner while we wait."

"I don't want to inconvenience you any further."

"I have to eat. And if Vance ever found out I'd left you alone, he'd have good cause to be furious. I'd expect him to do the same for Nancy if our positions were reversed."

Since she knew he spoke the truth, she gave in. They drove to the nearby Hilton. The next hour passed pleasantly as they enjoyed baked salmon, fresh asparagus and new potatoes in a marvelous wine sauce.

Libby listened with rapt attention as Peter related incidents from his university days, when he and Vance had met. The more he talked, the more she understood how much Vance had deprived both Peter and himself by ending their friendship over something to do with her. She tried to remember that night at the Anson estate. If Peter had been malicious or deliberately provocative, she would have been repulsed. But that hadn't been the case.

Throughout dessert, she found herself only half listening; her thoughts kept returning to Vance and his determination to end their marriage. But then Peter said something that caught her full attention. "You and Nancy lost a baby?" She mouthed the words on a tiny gasp as he told her the details.

Unexpectedly, he threw down his napkin. "Look, Libby. I didn't mean to talk you under the table."

"No, no," she hastened to reassure him. "That must have been agony for you. I'm so sorry."

"No more than what you and Vance are going through right now. He hides it well, but being blind must be hell on earth for him!"

Libby felt a sudden rush of tears and tried to fight them. "I'm sorry," Peter said, sounding distressed. "I shouldn't have mentioned it."

Libby shook her head. "I'm glad we had this talk. You've told me enough to convince me that you have nothing to do with the company's problems. But you hinted that you were onto something."

He pursed his lips. "Right—but until I'm certain of my facts, I'm not ready to lay my case before Vance. In any event, I doubt he'd give me the time of day. But that's not your worry. Shall we go?"

Libby rested her head against the window during the short drive to the service station. She felt fragmented. In addition to Peter's problems, she had to deal with the reality that Vance wanted her out of his house—and his life—tomorrow.

"Here we are, Libby. Safe and sound. It looks as if the Jeep is ready."

"Thank you for everything, Peter. I think it was providential bumping into you at the office."

"Thanks for listening." His mouth curved in a surprisingly gentle smile. "A rare virtue in anyone."

"Anytime."

"I think you mean that."

Libby jumped out of the truck and smiled up at him. "I plan to talk to Vance, you know."

He nodded, then with a quick wave of his hand, drove off. Libby hurriedly took care of the bill for the repairs and started out for the farm. It would be dark before much longer.

As soon as she turned the Jeep onto the dirt road, the perfume from the orange groves assailed her senses. How could he consider giving up the farm? And how could she bear to leave it? This was their home. And after the beauty of last night the idea of a divorce seemed to tear her heart from her body. If they hadn't made love last night, would he be asking her for a divorce today? What about the united front she and Vance were supposed to present to the world? Nothing made sense anymore....

"Where do you think you've been?"

Vance had unexpectedly opened the front door as she reached for the handle. She stepped back in shocked surprise. *He'd been waiting for her.* Martin must have told him she'd driven off with Peter. The strange expression on his face made her apprehensive.

"At a service station in Nairobi, waiting for the Jeep to be repaired." She started to walk past him, but he grasped her around the wrist and held her fast. Before she knew what had happened, he'd pinned her against the closed door, holding her arms so she couldn't move.

"And were you alone the entire time?" His face was so close, she could smell his after-shave and watch the little nerve that throbbed at the corner of his taut mouth. Last night they'd shared an experience so intense, she still trembled at the memory. Today, they'd reached a total impasse.

"Martin Dean didn't waste any time, did he? Peter was right." She knew the mention of his name would incense her husband, but at this point she didn't care. Things couldn't get any worse.

His mouth became a white line of fury. "The evidence against Peter is mounting by the minute. Do you realize he has no alibi for the night this house was set on fire? Can't you see how dangerous it is for you to be with him, under the present circumstances? I told you the night of the reception that I didn't trust him. Martin came to me with the news that you drove off with Peter because he was worried for you, and with good reason." His lips twisted menacingly. "So much for a loving, devoted sensible wife."

In a sudden burst of emotion, he crushed her body against him, lowering his mouth over hers, smothering any response she might have made. There was a desperation about the way he ravaged her lips, as if he were fighting some demon of his own tortured soul. He seemed bent on tormenting himself as well as her, yet the taste and feel of him drove everything else from her mind. She'd wanted this when she awakened this morning and found him gone. Needing the fulfillment that only he knew how to give, she moved closer to accommodate him. But as if he sensed her response, he pushed her swiftly away from him and took several steadying breaths. Libby rested against the door, trying to recover from the terrible disappointment of his unexpected reaction.

Vance placed his hands on his hips. "You have a very cavalier regard for your own safety, Libby."

"If you're still referring to Peter, you need to understand how that happened. He was at the elevator when I left your office and when he said he was going to the mine, I asked him if I could have a lift to the service station. He told me you wouldn't like it, that people would gossip. If you want the truth, I had to talk him into it."

He scowled. "Don't you see you were playing right into his hands? He *let* you talk him into it. Knowing I wouldn't like it, he *still* took the risk. The man has no conscience. More than ever, I want you out of Nairobi and back in England where you'll be safe. If you needed help with the Jeep, you should have told me."

"When I left your office, I wasn't thinking about the Jeep," she explained quietly. "Peter thought I was ill. He couldn't have been kinder and I certainly wasn't aware of any ulterior motives."

His face darkened. "Pleading his cause, Libby?"

"He explained what happened at your place in England three years ago, and I think there's something you should know."

"Are you trying to tell me Peter didn't do everything in his power to attract you that night? I was there. I saw it all." His eyes glittered with a dangerous light. "I didn't know I could be so wrong about a person."

"Yes. You saw it all. But you don't know the reason for what he did."

His face clouded over. "What are you talking about?"

"He did it as a joke, Vance. Nancy was in on it," she said, warming to the subject. "They'd begun to wonder if you and I were in love. Peter thought he knew you better than anyone, and he was surprised to think it might be true, so he put their idea to the test."

Vance closed his eyes, but she could tell he had started to listen.

"The problems began when his suspicions turned out to be correct. In finding out what he wanted to know, he lost your respect and your friendship. Don't you see? That's why Nancy took me shopping. She wanted to explain. But when she realized that I'd been unaware of any byplay, there was nothing to say."

He muttered something unintelligible. "He really got to you, didn't he?"

"You couldn't be more wrong," she lamented. "I asked him about that night. He would never have brought up the subject otherwise. Why didn't you let him explain what happened? You've hurt him and yourself by not allowing him his day in court. I have a feeling the only thing Peter's guilty of is an innocent joke that somehow backfired. And now his marriage and his career have all but been destroyed."

Vance didn't move. "You'd make a top-notch barrister. My congratulations. Your defense of his total innocence is brilliant. The master touch. He found the perfect advocate in you, my precious wife."

She smoothed the hair back from her forehead. "He needs someone who'll listen to him. It's obvious that coming to you would be a gesture in futility."

"Martin's wife could enlighten you about the noble Peter Fromms. You don't have to take my word for it."

Libby's chin lifted. "For your information, Peter's still in love with his wife. The man's suffering, Vance. He spent most of the time at dinner reminiscing about their marriage and—"

"Dinner?"

"Yes. We ate dinner together while I waited for the Jeep to be repaired. He refused to let me stay by myself. During the course of the conversation, he told me about the baby they lost, and—"

"Baby," he interjected, rubbing his neck absently. "What baby?"

"Nancy had a miscarriage at six months. Peter said it practically destroyed both of them for a while."

Silence filled the hallway. "And when was this supposed to have happened?"

Libby folded her arms, remembering the sadness in Peter's voice. "I don't know exactly. I think he said about two years ago...but I could be wrong. Quite frankly, I'm amazed he's continued to work for you at all. Right now, he's following up some leads concerning the cave-in."

Vance inclined his head toward her. "He sucked you in completely. He wants something from you, Libby. Mark my words. I wouldn't be surprised if he just happened to drop by here on the way back from the mine—to see if you're safe. Any pretext to get at me."

"Is there no reasoning with you? The man admits he made a ghastly error in judgment. Doesn't he deserve a fair hearing? Think, Vance—he was your best friend!"

"*Was* being the operative word."

Libby closed her eyes in despair at his stubbornness. She would have retorted, but a knock at the front door prevented her from saying anything further. Vance let out a harsh laugh.

"What did I tell you? My best friend couldn't even make it to the mine before turning back, and why not? He knows he's welcome here." In his anger, he brushed past Libby and jerked open the front door. "What do you want, Fromms?"

The lanky farm manager stood in the doorway, holding his hat. "It's James, Mr. Anson. Sorry to bother you, but Diablo has a swelling on his leg that I thought you'd want to know about. He's running a temperature, as well."

Vance handled his mistake with remarkable aplomb, but Libby watched the dark red flush stain his cheeks. "Sorry about that, James. I'll meet you at the barn in a moment." The other man nodded, tipping his head to Libby in greeting as he turned to walk away.

"The evening's still young," Vance added pointedly, "and we're by no means through with this conversation."

When he'd stormed out of the farmhouse, Libby decided to leave for Nairobi immediately, before he came back. She had an idea that Vance wouldn't be satisfied until he'd personally escorted her onto the plane and fastened her seat belt for her.

With firm resolve, she went to the bedroom to pack a suitcase, grabbing a few clothes, enough to see her through the next week—until she could work out a plan. For the second time that day, she started the Jeep and headed for the city. If the new Stanley Hotel didn't have a room, she'd try the Hilton. It was the height of the tourist season, which could conceivably be a problem, but she'd worry about that later. Telling Vance about Peter had only increased his determination to make her leave—the one thing she had no intention of doing.

CHAPTER NINE

"JAMBO," LIBBY TRIED OUT one of the few Swahili words she'd learned on the bank teller.

"Jambo," the woman answered back with a warm smile.

After that greeting, Libby quickly reverted to English and collected the money she'd asked her stepfather to wire her the night before.

En route to the hotel, she wandered in and out of the main bazaar. Her interest was caught by some hand carvings, and she ended up buying one, the head of a proud Bantu warrior. Something about the firm jawline and steady eyes reminded her of Vance.

Her purse held a brochure she'd picked up that morning on a city tour through the university area. She planned to study the syllabus of classes available to foreigners as soon as she returned to her hotel room.

She didn't see how Vance could object to her enrolling in a few classes on the African language. After all, she'd graduated from the International School with a language degree. A course or two would help fill the time until she could find a way to make Vance change his mind.

She'd also approach a reputable realtor to help her look for a rental flat in a good area of the city. Living out of a hotel room would not only be expensive, but impersonal. A flat would give her a sense of permanence and show Vance that she meant to make their marriage work.

Libby entered the lobby of the New Stanley Hotel a little after six and inquired at the desk about any messages. She'd left word with the concierge at Vance's flat to have Charles phone her. Someone had to make sure Vance saw the doctor. The severity of his headaches convinced Libby he needed to be examined. The fall he'd taken that day they went horseback riding could have caused more damage so soon after the other injury. But short of drugging her husband, she didn't know how to get him to Dr. Stillman's office.

"It's about time. James dropped me off hours ago!"

Vance's tall frame dominated the hotel room as Libby let herself inside. She wasn't totally surprised to see him, and braced herself for the worst.

"You might have had the decency to let me know you were leaving the farm last night."

She could tell he was furious, although he held himself in check. "Since I'd already told you I'd be staying at the hotel, I didn't see the necessity. To be truthful, I thought it best to leave immediately, so there wouldn't be a scene in front of Charles this morning."

Vance didn't move a muscle, but his face might have been chiseled out of solid granite. In a charcoal-gray suit and waistcoat, he looked more imposing than usual.

"Where have you been all day? The manager of the hotel said you left before eight this morning."

Her heart gave a little kick. Dared she hope he'd been worried about her? "I decided to see the sights of Nairobi."

"On your own?" His mouth hardened.

"With a tour group. It's something I've wanted to do ever since I came to Kenya."

The pulse at his temple throbbed. "You missed today's flight, but I've made another reservation for tomorrow." He reached into his pocket and pulled out the hated airline ticket. "I expect you to be on it. Charles will escort you and help you with your bags. He'll also take the opportunity to discuss the divorce with you."

"I won't be here." She plucked the ticket from his hand and put it back in his suitcoat pocket. "You keep it. I have no use for it."

He was like a bomb, ready to explode. "If you refuse to fly home, then you're completely on your own."

"I'm a grown woman, Vance. And a married one."

"Nairobi is no place for a beautiful woman on her own. You're completely unfamiliar with the city. You'll be fair game."

"That's my concern."

"This isn't London, Libby." His voice was deceptively quiet.

"According to the registrar at the university, many single people attend classes and live in flats near the campus. Apparently they manage just fine in this great big, wicked city."

His brows were a dark line of disbelief. "I hope you're not saying what—"

A sudden rapping at the door caused him to pause midsentence. Libby rushed to answer it, thankful for the diversion.

"Charles! Come in!" she called out gladly, kissing him on the cheek as he breezed through the doorway carrying his briefcase, his jacket draped over one arm.

"Good. You're both here." He smiled knowingly at Libby, then patted Vance on the shoulder. Libby took his things and put them on one of the twin beds. "I have news, but if I'm interrupting, I'll come back."

"No, no. Sit down. I've been waiting for you to get in touch with me," Libby assured him. "Why don't I call room service? We can eat dinner while we talk. Use the bathroom to freshen up while I see about our meal, if you want."

"Thanks, my dear." Charles strode from the room while Libby reached for the phone to place their order.

Out of the corner of her eye she watched Vance as he felt for a chair. He shrugged out of his suit jacket and vest, hanging them both on the back of the rattan chair. The tie went next. Libby replaced the receiver, enjoying the look of him. She felt a quickening in her body. His nearness would always affect her like this.

"We haven't finished our conversation yet, Libby. So don't get any ideas about my leaving with Charles when he's ready to go," he threatened.

"Why would I do that? I want you to stay," she said with a sense of great daring, and had the satisfaction of watching his knuckles turn white as he gripped the edge of the chair.

"You left a suitcase in my office yesterday. I brought it here and put it in the closet. Since you refuse to leave Nairobi, I have to wonder why you bothered to pack that bag."

"When I came to your office, I hoped we might go to dinner at a hotel, dance, talk...stay the night." Her voice trailed off.

Before Vance had a chance to respond, Charles came back into the room and told them to gather round. He had his shirtsleeves rolled up, ready for work. By the look on Vance's face, Libby could tell that her explanation was the last thing he'd expected to hear. He'd never know how the scene in his office yesterday had devastated her.

Charles's next words returned her to the present. "Have you told Elizabeth what we've uncovered?"

A silence pervaded the room. "No. Not yet."

Charles's thick brows lifted in question as he eyed Libby.

"Were you able to listen to McPherson's tape?" Vance asked the older man.

"I did more than that. I turned it in to the board a few minutes ago. That's the reason I'm late getting back here," he explained. His gray eyes were alive with excitement as he sat down in a chair opposite Libby. "Everything has fallen into place much sooner than I expected, mostly thanks to you, Libby. Vance's troubles are almost over."

Libby leaned forward, a stunned expression on her face. "What did I do?" The good news hadn't started to sink in yet.

"You tell her, Vance. After all, if you hadn't acted on the information Libby gave you, it might have taken us weeks to learn what we know now."

The shuttered expression on Vance's face told Libby he didn't relish the idea of explaining anything to her. Under the circumstances, she would have thought he'd be overjoyed to know there was hope!

Finally he said, "If you recall a certain conversation we had about Peter last evening, you'll remember telling me about a baby they lost. When you told me it happened two years ago, it sparked something in my memory." He paused. "I decided to call Nancy in Perth."

Libby bowed her head, waiting for the rest of his story in breathless anticipation.

"Not only were you correct in everything you said about Peter, I also found out why Nancy left him. They quarreled bitterly over Martin Dean's attempt to blackmail Peter. That, plus more importantly, the loss of the baby, influenced Nancy to leave Nairobi for a time and try to get things in perspective."

"Blackmail?" Her eyes grew round in amazement. "Martin blackmailed Peter?"

Vance ran both hands through his hair wearily, as if he had trouble admitting the rest. "My rules on company behavior are rigid, Libby. No alcohol while on duty. No exceptions. One evening two years ago, Peter did have a few drinks because he'd just found out that Nancy had lost the baby. He wasn't on duty, of course, but an emergency cropped up at the mine. As Chief Engineer he was called to take care of it. I was in London at the time." He paced restlessly.

"It seems that Peter went to work and took care of the problem in spite of the pain he was in. He also surprised Martin Dean in the company office at midnight. Martin was looking over some blueprints that he had no business seeing at all. Blueprints for the Naivasha mine, I might add. No one but Peter and myself had access to those papers. Peter confronted him. That's when Martin threatened to come to me about Peter's drinking problem. He knew I'd fire Peter if I found out. At least, he believed I would."

Libby could see it all clearly.

"To make a long story short," Vance went on, "Peter didn't report Martin, but he told Nancy what had happened. She begged Peter to talk to me about it."

"And did he?" Libby asked.

"No. He was too afraid." And they both knew why. "He didn't tell me about the night Martin sent him on a wild-goose chase, either. The night my farm was burned."

"How horrible for Peter."

"Right." He grimaced. "After that, Martin started dropping hints about Peter's drinking bouts. Word spread like wildfire."

"When in reality he rarely drinks," Libby added. "He didn't order wine or beer with our meal yesterday."

Vance pushed himself away from the table with a tortured expression on his face. "Nancy could see what was going on, and begged Peter to come forward, but he refused. He felt that if he watched Martin carefully in time he could catch him out."

"Oh, Vance—" Compassion laced her words. "The poor man."

Vance nodded. "Martin told me Peter had started making advances toward his wife, and like a fool, I believed him."

"Because of the way you thought he'd come on to me," she said slowly. "What a tragedy."

In an unexpected movement, Vance got up from the table and clutched the chair for support. "When time came for promotions, I moved Martin to chief engineer, and put Peter on probation, demoting him to a junior position until he could prove himself again. I never believed that he would. Nancy was furious with Peter by then, because he wouldn't do anything to help himself. She threatened to leave him, hoping that might make the difference. But he hung on because he hoped that in the end, the truth would win out.'' Vance's voice cracked with emotion.

"And it has!" Libby cried out joyfully.

He turned his head in her direction. "But not without its consequences.''

"Peter probably felt too far down and thought Nancy would be better off without him," she mused.

"Nancy's words exactly. You're a very intuitive woman, Libby.''

She gave a sad little laugh. "Not intuitive, Vance. From what I've observed in my life, people have a tendency to give up when the going gets rough.'' Her eyes locked with Charles's. He'd been a silent witness for quite some time.

A loud knock had Vance answering the door before Libby could even get to her feet. A waiter brought in their dinner. She watched Vance tip the man and then show him out. Her husband behaved almost as naturally as a sighted person. It occurred to her that Vance had adapted well to his dark world. If only the headaches would go away...

"This looks delicious," Charles murmured, pouring wine into the long-stemmed glasses as Libby put Vance's dinner before him. "The beautiful thing is that Nancy allowed Vance to tape their conversation, Libby. She'll be flying to Nairobi to testify under oath at the official hearing.''

"But that's wonderful. Does Peter know?''

"He knows," Vance muttered. "We spent all night talking." Libby waited for him to finish. "We've made our peace. I have you to thank for that, Libby, and a great deal more. Apparently Martin has nursed a growing hatred for me for the past several years. You turned everything around when you championed Peter. That's when I finally learned about Martin's sick jealousy."

Her eyes filled with tears. "I'm so glad. Peter cares for you a great deal. I think he's a wonderful person."

Vance cleared his throat. "I agree. Thank God you stood up for him," he said fervently in a rare display of gratitude—rare since his blindness, Libby amended.

"Amen," Charles added warmly. "Because of Nancy and Peter's combined testimony, I'll be able to depose others within the company. Add to that certain discrepancies I discovered as I circulated at the reception, and it appears all roads lead to one man."

"Martin," Libby stated quietly.

Vance nodded. "Primarily, but also Ralphs, Fogarty and possibly several others. I'm going to enjoy knowing they're well and truly caught. All of them gave depositions before I ever left the hospital. At this point, those depos are so full of holes, none of them has a leg to stand on."

Libby covered his hand, forgetting for a moment the enmity between them. "You must be the happiest man alive right now, Vance." The tears slid down her cheeks but she didn't care if Charles saw them. "You weren't really going to sell the farm to Martin."

After a slight pause, Vance pulled his hand away on the pretext of drinking his wine. "Yes, Libby. Now that I'm blind, there's no point in keeping the farm. I can't work it or enjoy it as I did in the past. However, as far as Martin's concerned, my offer to give him first option to buy still stands. I don't want him catching wind of anything yet. After he and the others are brought in for questioning and subsequently charged, I'll put it on the market again. He's had my confidence for a long time. I'll dangle him a while longer until the case is closed." She heard the finality in his words and a new sadness entered her heart.

"Do you have definite proof that he caused the disaster?" she asked, trying to conceal the fresh pain she felt.

"We do," Charles interjected, turning sympathetic eyes on her. "McPherson was the foreman on duty the night that Peter allegedly drank on duty. He saw Martin and Ralphs enter the office without authorization—not only then, but on numerous other occasions. Martin threatened his family with bodily harm if he talked. McPherson also saw Martin enter the Naivashu mine right before the cave-in, but was terrified to come forward for fear of reprisal. Peter went to the mine last night and talked McPherson into coming forward with the truth, *which he put on tape.* We've got him, my dear." A wide smile broke out on Charles's face.

Vance stirred restlessly. "Martin removed those timbers before the charges were set off. He figured Peter would be blamed."

"Martin made one too many mistakes," Charles added. "If you remember, Libby, I went off with a group of people to his house the night of the reception. He'd had too much to drink already. A few more when we arrived at his place and he started in on Fromms. He didn't have a good thing to say about him. He might have taken me in if he hadn't dwelt exclusively on Peter's faults and his way with the ladies. When your name was mentioned, my dear Elizabeth, I knew the man to be a liar."

"I should have seen it ages ago," Vance agonized aloud. "What a fool I've been!"

Libby's gaze met Charles's in a moment of perfect understanding. By now, Charles had to know about Vance's hostility toward Peter—that his mistaken conception of what took place in London three years before had helped lay the groundwork for the trouble in his company.

"In all fairness, Vance," she hastened to say, "if our positions had been reversed and I'd seen Nancy really trying to play up to you, I might have poisoned her martini."

Charles's deep-throated chuckle defused a potentially explosive moment. Vance frowned, rubbing his forehead with a distracted hand.

"You know," she added, "I thought Martin behaved strangely the first time I met him. He kept staring at Vance and me. I thought it was because he'd been hurt by Vance's keeping the news of our marriage from him. Something like that. Now that we know the truth, it seems to me he's bitterly jealous of you, Vance, not only for your accomplishments, but for other reasons, too. For the respect and love you inspire in other people. He could never compete with that. Your blindness made no difference to the way your employees and your colleagues—and your wife— feel about you. And I think that shocked him."

"I couldn't have put it better myself." Charles reached across the table and gripped her hand firmly.

"That envy has led him and other men I trusted to commit murder, and they're going to pay dearly," Vance vowed in a fierce tone that made Libby shiver.

"That's right," Charles concurred, as he got up from the table to stretch his legs. "As a precaution, I've had the committee put all those involved under surveillance till the hearing. They're dead men if they make one more wrong move."

Charles gathered up his jacket and briefcase. "If you two will excuse me, I'm going back to the flat to phone Marion. Tonight I can give her the good news that you're cleared, Vance, and that I'll be flying home shortly. All's well that ends well—as the poet said." He gave Vance another pat on the shoulder. "You've had a hell of a time up to now, but the worst is behind you."

"Let me see you out." Libby stood up from the table and walked him to the door. Vance remained seated, waiting to resume his attack on her.

"I'll see you in the morning," Charles murmured. "Be ready by seven." He kissed her on the cheek and walked purposefully down the corridor. She realized that Charles would follow Vance's instructions out of loyalty.

Libby closed the door behind him. *Charles couldn't do anything if he couldn't find her in the morning—and Vance wouldn't be able to blame him.* She whirled around and eyed her husband shrewdly. The situation demanded new tactics.

"He's gone."

"Yes. As you've heard for yourself, your presence at my side is no longer required. I'm divorcing you, Libby. If you try to resist me, you'll wish you hadn't."

She took a steadying breath. "I'm not resisting anymore. You can have your divorce. I'll agree to anything you want."

Not by as much as the twitch of a muscle, did Vance let on that her words surprised him, but the color drained from his face. "You mean that?" he asked hoarsely.

"Just don't ask me to give back my engagement ring. It's the one memory that will always stand out in my mind—the night you asked me to marry you. That kind of joy only comes once in a lifetime."

Pulling off the gold wedding band, Libby walked over to Vance and pressed it into his hand, lying palm upward on the table. When she looked into his face, she could see no expression at all.

In a convulsive movement, his fingers closed over the ring and he dropped it into his shirt pocket. The simple act severed the minute hope that her husband would relent and let her be a wife to him. His determination to go his way alone staggered her.

"What will you do, Libby?" he asked at last, breaking the long, painful silence.

Her chin lifted. "That's no concern of yours anymore. You've provided me with an airline ticket, so I believe that's everything. The rest is up to Charles, isn't it?" She watched the way his hands gripped the edge of the table. "If a child results from our one night together, do you want to be informed or not?"

"Libby!"

She drew a deep breath, pleased to see that he wasn't as self-controlled as she'd supposed.

"As you said, it's only a possibility. I'm simply trying to cover every eventuality since this is the last time we'll ever see each other."

Slowly, Vance got to his feet and reached behind him for his vest and jacket, but he moved like a man thirty years older. "If there is a child, get in touch with Charles and a trust fund will be established."

Taking her courage in both hands, she ventured, "And when I marry again, do you prefer the child to retain your name, or will it matter? There are a lot of men who want to adopt the child they'll be raising."

His mouth became a thin line of rage as he jerked into his clothes, stuffing the tie in his pocket. "Why this obsession with a baby that, for all intents and purposes, doesn't even exist?"

Libby smiled. "You didn't answer my question. I'd like all the legal ends tied up now, Vance. I don't want to have to make an unnecessary trip to Nairobi at some future date because of a technicality."

His pale face contorted with anger. "Charles will see to all the legalities." He started feeling his way to the door.

"Then there's nothing more to say. Goodbye, Vance."

He reached for the door handle. "Libby..." he grated. He seemed to have trouble articulating. "Before I go, is there anything you need?"

Anything I need? Libby stared at her husband incredulously. "My freedom will do."

His chest rose and fell. "Will you live in London with your parents?"

She eyed him narrowly. "Probably not. But surely my plans for the future have nothing to do with you. Unless you're asking me not to leave you, I think this should be goodbye."

Abruptly he wrenched open the door. He walked unsteadily away from her, feeling the wall until he came to the elevator. Libby stood in the doorway and watched her husband until he disappeared from sight. Concern for his safety led her to call the desk and ask them to assist Mr. Anson to a taxi. She couldn't tell whether his ashen color was due to one of his headaches or to the fact that she was leaving him. In any case, he looked ill and her fear grew.

Until tonight, she'd never purposely deceived Vance. He'd believed her when she said she'd be leaving in the morning. But she couldn't possibly go away. He was her life; a future without him was unthinkable.

Full of renewed determination, she hurried to the closet and pulled out her suitcases, including the one Vance had brought from his office. It didn't take long to pack since she hadn't yet put her things away in drawers. Her glance about the room took in the head of the Bantu warrior she'd purchased at the bazaar. She quickly wrapped it inside a sweater and buried it between layers of clothes for safekeeping. With that accomplished, she locked her cases and went down to the lobby to check out and pay the bill. While she waited, she tore up the airline ticket and threw the remains in a nearby wastebasket.

Within a half hour, Libby had checked into the Hilton Hotel, where she'd had dinner with Peter. The only room left was the bridal suite—an irony—but she took it. As far as she knew, no one in the world had any idea where she was at that moment, which suited her just fine.

She had room service deliver some juice, then she wandered out to the small patio adjoining her suite. The night was cool, but not uncomfortably so. Sitting down on one of the lounge chairs, she looked out over the city from five stories up. She'd never felt so alone.

For an hour or more, Libby stared into the night, while an enormous yellow moon rose higher in the sky. In time, she reflected, she'd find a way to approach Vance—to make their marriage real. No matter what, she could never walk away from him. He needed her, though he still refused to believe it. And she needed him that much more.

She sipped her drink until the air grew too chilly, then went in to bed. Tomorrow she'd look for a flat and register for some classes. But before she did that, she'd have to make contact with Charles and explain to him why she left the hotel without telling anyone. And right now, Charles was her only hope of making Vance see reason where his health was concerned.

The next morning, Libby ate breakfast in her room while she put through a phone call to Charles. There was no answer at the flat. She decided to try again in half an hour. Still no response. By now, he would have realized that she was hiding from him.

For the next two hours, Libby tried unsuccessfully to reach him. There was the distinct possibility that he'd gone to Vance's office to tell him she'd disappeared. Libby didn't dare call there under the circumstances.

At noon, she took a taxi from the Hilton to the New Stanley, hoping to find out if he'd been there or left any messages for her.

"Charles?" Even from behind, she recognized his iron-gray hair and she hurried toward him. He was talking to the day clerk, obviously upset.

His frown evaporated when he heard her voice. "Libby!" he cried, putting down his briefcase to hug her hard. "Where have you been? I've searched everywhere for you. The airport, the railway station, the rental car places. I couldn't imagine what had happened to you when I found out you'd checked out of the hotel last night. My darling girl—you've given me the worst six hours of my entire life."

Guilt washed over her in waves. Charles had a pallor she'd never seen before. "I'm sorry," she began breathlessly, "but I had no intention of flying back to London this morning or discussing a divorce. Vance thinks I've gone, but I could no more leave him than I could stop breathing. I love him, Charles—" she started to break down "—a-and I didn't want him to blame you for not carrying out his orders, so I thought that if you couldn't find me—"

"Libby," he murmured, enfolding her in his arms. The comfort he offered was her undoing, and she sobbed quietly into his shoulder, oblivious to the stares of interested hotel guests. "He's really put you through it, hasn't he?" The question didn't demand an answer. He handed her a snowy-white handkerchief. "Use this."

"I know he loves me, Charles," she said as she wiped her eyes. "If only he'd give our marriage a chance. And I'm so worried about his headaches, I can't sleep at night. He needs to see the doctor, but he's so stubborn. If he keeps this up, he won't be well enough to run his company. The headaches are increasing.... If you can't persuade him, maybe I should call his father. Winslow would fly here on the next plane. Vance has got to listen to someone!"

Charles patted her head. "Come and sit down with me." He ushered Libby to a banquette against the wall of the foyer, clasping her cold hands in his. Libby looked up and saw compassion shining from his eyes.

"I have something to tell you, Libby. I'm breaking a confidence, but you're entitled to know the truth so that you can have some peace. No one deserves it more than you."

"Something's happened to Vance!" she cried out as fear quickened her heartbeat. "Don't keep anything from me, Charles."

"Libby—" he leaned forward "—Vance went into the hospital late last night."

"I knew something like this would happen." The tears started again. She moved to get up, but he held her hands in a firm grip.

"Hear me out," he admonished kindly. "The other day at the flat, a headache hit Vance so hard, he blacked out for a few seconds. When I told him I was calling for an ambulance he told me he'd already been to the doctor and knew what was causing the pain.

"New X rays were taken during his checkup. It seems that the tiny ore fragment inside his head has shifted, and this is why he's had those excruciating head pains. Because of its new position, the doctor said he could operate to remove the fragment. Vance is in surgery right now."

"I don't believe it." She shook her head dazedly, trying to take it all in.

"It's true." He smiled and let go of her hands. "Vance didn't want you to know anything about it. Whatever went on between the two of you after I left the hotel last night, he decided to have the operation. Apparently the doctor wanted to operate several days ago."

Libby closed her eyes, wondering what it all meant.

"Vance went under the anesthetic this morning, believing that you were on a plane back to England. If he had any idea you were still here—that you knew about this—it might affect his recovery. Do you understand what I'm saying?"

"Then he thinks you saw me off at the airport this morning? You didn't tell him?" she asked in awe.

Charles shook his gray head. "I lied to him exactly the way you did, my dear. He believes you gave him his divorce and that you've gone out of his life forever. When you weren't in your room this morning, I had an idea you'd disappeared on purpose. I was anxious to reach you—to tell you about Vance."

Libby looked at him with pleading eyes. "What am I going to do? I can't leave him!"

He sighed. "I never believed you could or would. But for the time being, he mustn't know you're here. My advice, for what it's worth, is to stay close by and fight. As far as I can tell, you're winning all the time."

She lifted a ravaged face to him. "How can you say that when he thinks I've agreed to a divorce?"

"I can say that because I've known Vance for years. When he called me after the accident, I didn't give your marriage a prayer of surviving. To be frank, I didn't expect to find you in Kenya. You see, he told me about the strong letter he sent you, giving you your marching papers."

"I would have ignored that letter and come anyway," Libby asserted.

"I believe you," he said, chuckling. "Nevertheless, Vance was as determined as I've ever seen him in my life that your marriage was finished. And then, to my wondering surprise—" he paused and grinned at her "—I discovered you ensconced at the farmhouse. Vance had enlisted your help and was acting very much like a husband by the time I arrived.''

"He only allowed me to stay because you told him to." Her voice trembled with remembered pain. "To give the illusion of a united front."

Strong hands gripped her shoulders, forcing her to look at him. "That's where you're wrong, Libby. I told him no such thing. In fact, I was secretly relieved that you weren't in Nairobi. With the mess he was in, I feared for your safety almost as much as he did. But he found a way to keep you with him—without admitting that he wanted his wife."

Libby stared at him for a full minute as the significance of what he said started to sink in. A smile lifted the corners of her mouth until it radiated from her whole face.

"Thank you for telling me that, Charles." She hugged him fiercely. "I needed to hear that, more than you know."

His smile faded. "Vance would have my head, Libby."

She sobered. "I know."

His shrewd gaze played over her delicate features. "There's something else you should know, but Dr. Stillman will have to be the one to tell you. Why don't you go over to the hospital right now and I'll join you in an hour or so?"

"Thank you, Charles." She pressed a kiss to his cheek, then hurried outside to get a taxi. Her heart pounded sickeningly in her breast. *What didn't she know?* If the doctor needed to talk to her, it had to mean bad news. Libby hid her face in her hands, almost immobilized with fear. Was Vance's life jeopardized in some way because of this latest development? She couldn't lose him now. She couldn't!

CHAPTER TEN

"MRS. ANSON?" The large man in the surgical mask walked toward Libby as she paced back and forth in the waiting room. She didn't recognize him until he untied it.

"Oh, Dr. Stillman. Thank goodness."

"I understood you'd gone back to England."

Libby moistened her dry lips. "Vance thinks I have, but I had to find out how he is. Charles told me about the operation, but he said you had something important to tell me. Please—how's Vance? I have to know."

"The operation was a complete success."

"Thank God," she whispered. "I begged him to keep that appointment with you last week, but he wouldn't listen. His headaches kept getting worse and worse."

"It's a good thing they did. Otherwise, it would have been too late."

Libby felt dizzy. "Too late? You mean he might have died?" she cried out. She leaned heavily against the arm that went around her shoulders.

"Come and sit down." He led her to the nearest chair. "Your husband obviously didn't want you to know about his condition. What *has* he told you?"

"Nothing. But anyone could see he's been in excruciating pain since his fall."

"He didn't tell you the outcome of his checkup with me last week?"

Libby shook her head. "I didn't even know he had one until Charles—Mr. Rankin—told me."

His eyes narrowed. "Then Mr. Rankin probably explained that the blow to the head your husband received while you were out riding caused the ore fragment to move. That's why he started having such severe pain. It's also the reason you noticed him covering his eyes. You see, when the fragment was resting in its original place, it was in an inoperable position. The optic nerve appeared to be damaged. But when it moved out of that position, the X ray revealed that the nerve might have been kinked, rather than severed. Some light started getting through the nerve after he fell."

"Which meant the nerve wasn't severed!" Libby burst out, getting to her feet.

He smiled. "That's right, Mrs. Anson. But I didn't know until I operated if the nerve was damaged or not. The chances of it being left intact were slight . . . and I explained this to your husband. At first, he couldn't see the point of undergoing surgery for a procedure with no guarantees. He opted to live with the headaches . . . until last night. I received a phone call from him quite late. He told me he'd changed his mind and wanted to have the surgery as soon as possible."

Libby clutched her hands to her chest. "Tell me what you found?" she managed to ask in a small voice.

He got up from his chair and walked over to her. "Exactly what I'd hoped to find. I'm not always right, but this was one of those rare occasions. The nerve was kinked, but the good news is that not a single thread was broken. The odds against that happening are a million to one, you realize."

"Doctor!"

"Put out your hand, Mrs. Anson."

Libby did as she was told, lifting a trembling hand toward him. He pulled something from his surgery smock...a minute, diamond-shaped ore fragment. "I believe this is a souvenir you'll want to hang on to."

She stared at it, then closed her fingers around it. This tiny piece of metal had entered Vance's skull and deprived him of his sight. Now she held it in the palm of her hand. Incredible! She had an idea what she was going to do with it, and lifted her head. "Does this mean his sight will be restored?"

Dr. Stillman sighed deeply. "That remains to be seen. The nerve has been in a kinked position for more than a month. I had to straighten it. And now, it will take time to start functioning again. It may not regenerate any further than it already has done. In other words, your husband may always be blind, but remain sensitive to light, as you've already seen."

"But if it does come back, how soon will he see?"

"That's hard to tell. A week—ten days, maybe. Certainly no earlier than that. Now we begin a waiting game. But remember, I can guarantee nothing."

"I know, but to have a chance at all is still a miracle to me."

"The miracle is that he hit his head the way he did. Without that blow, the fragment would have stayed put, pressing permanently against the nerve. If we hadn't operated soon, it would have been too late for the regeneration process. You know, Mrs. Anson, I'd almost say you were pushed into your husband by an unseen hand. How fortunate for him that it happened."

"I can't believe any of this. Vance has kept me completely in the dark."

"I'm aware of that. And because of the delicate nature of this operation and the recovery period, I'd rather he didn't find out you were still here, or that you know anything. I don't want his recuperation jeopardized by emotional trauma of any kind. The mind and the will play an incalculable part in the recovery process. Your presence could remind him of what he had to give up with the loss of his sight. It could cause him to lose ground at the very moment he must fight to win."

He put a gentle hand on her arm. "You're welcome to be here, to stay in his room—but don't make a sound, don't let on that you're there. I'll warn the staff to ignore you. When the bandages come off and we see the final results, then you can continue the battle." His eyes were twinkling as he spoke.

Libby started to laugh through the tears. She couldn't help it. "It's more like all-out war, doctor."

He grinned. "But you're still here fighting," he said, giving her arm a reassuring squeeze. "Now if you'll excuse me, I've got several other patients to see whose prognosis isn't anything like your husband's."

Libby grasped his large hand in both of hers. "Thank you. What an inadequate word..."

"He'll be in the recovery room until nine, maybe later. Why don't you grab a bite to eat and relax? There's quite a wait yet." He patted her shoulder and turned in the direction of the nursing station down the hall.

Deciding to take his advice, she found the cafeteria and ate an early dinner to fortify herself. Maybe Vance wouldn't get his sight back, she mused. But at least he'd be out of pain.

Suddenly, she couldn't keep the news to herself any longer, and left the cafeteria in search of a phone. It didn't matter if she wakened everyone. Vance needed the prayers of the people who loved him.

First, she phoned Vance's father. They were both so overcome that there was little conversation for a few minutes. The talk with her parents proved to be equally emotional. Libby promised to call them when she knew anything else. She stressed that they were not to phone Vance.

Charles was pacing back and forth at the nursing station when Libby arrived on Vance's floor. She reached for his hand and held it fast. He stayed with her for several hours; now and then, they talked quietly, but most of the time they waited in companionable silence, sitting in the private room Vance would occupy. Close to nine, Charles announced he would have to leave, explaining he still had several documents to prepare for the next day. She hugged him tightly, her heart so full of gratitude and hope that she couldn't speak.

At nine-thirty, Libby heard a noise outside Vance's private room. She stood up in nervous anticipation as his trolley was wheeled in. Her eyes went to her husband lying there helpless, and her heart swelled with love for him. His nose and mouth looked dark and bruised against the white gauze wrapped around his head and eyes like a turban. The distinct odors of the operating room clung to his body and to the sheets covering him. If Dr. Stillman hadn't already assured her of the operation's success, she'd have been alarmed at the way Vance looked. Instead, she felt relaxed and at peace for the first time since that day at White Oaks, when she had learned of his accident. She still shuddered as she recalled that nightmarish moment. How far removed from this wonderful day.

Near midnight she noticed indications that he was coming around. The nurse had taken his vital signs earlier, but he'd remained motionless. Now he was restless, making small, unintelligible noises. Libby pressed the button on the wall, summoning the matron. In a moment, Mrs. Grady, looking efficient and spanking fresh in her white uniform, entered the room and walked briskly over to Vance.

"There now, Mr. Anson." She took his hand in both of hers. "It's all right, you'll see." His speech gradually became more audible, and his hand clung to hers, filling Libby with a terrible envy.

"What's happening?" he whispered. "All those colors—my head is filled with them. Libby? Libby?" he cried out urgently, and it was almost her undoing. She wanted to cover him with her body, merge with him, give him all the love and strength that was in her. "Libby, darling—the colors," he muttered, his agitation obvious.

"You're all right." Mrs. Grady's tone was gentle. She bestowed a speaking look on Libby, who stood at the other side of the bed. "The operation is over, Mr. Anson, and successful it was, too. You'll be right as rain. You'll see." She stroked his hands. Her tenderness seemed to quiet him and he slept.

The fact that he'd called her name and whispered endearments in those first few minutes was all that sustained Libby for the following three days. She was forced to keep a silent vigil as Dr. Stillman, various nurses, Charles and Peter were all allowed to talk to him, touch him, give him encouragement. She almost broke down when the two widows they'd visited at the village came to pay their respects.

Libby slept at the hotel, then slipped back into his room before he awakened in the mornings. She could never get enough of him, never stop feasting her eyes on his beloved face. The first days of discomfort from the surgery passed, and Libby could see that Vance experienced a feeling of well-being. He talked about images and colors going constantly through his head. Dr. Stillman explained to her in private that it meant his sight was returning. It might come any day now. Whether it would be partial or a full restoration was anyone's guess.

Later in the week, the doctor removed the bandages. Libby sat in a chair with her hands clasped rigidly in her lap.

"All right, Vance. The last of the gauze is about to come off. Don't expect to see anything yet. It's still too soon. I'm going to give you a pair of specially treated glasses. You'll wear them during the day, take them off at night while you sleep. Any questions?"

"None." With that one word, Libby could sense how great was the tension that gripped him. The waiting had begun....

Her gaze fastened on the doctor's hands as the turban fell away, revealing her husband's dark brown hair with a shaved patch where the incision had been made. Dr. Stillman examined the wound, put on a new dressing, then handed Vance the glasses, which he put on.

"How do you feel?" He took Vance's pulse.

"Like a weight has just been lifted."

"The head is sensitive to any excess weight or pressure. Move slowly for the next few hours, to adjust to the light-headed feeling."

She heard Vance sigh. "How long do you think it will be before there's a change in my vision? If any," he added in a low voice. Libby bit her lip, wishing she could comfort him.

"That, Mr. Anson, is up to Mother Nature. Every person's timetable is different. This afternoon, the nurse will walk with you down the corridor and back. As your body returns to its normal activity, so will your eyes. This is the hardest time, Vance. Don't be too impatient. Don't do too much thinking. Listen to the radio or television. Ask your friends to read to you."

"I think I'll dispense with the latter," Vance drawled in shades of his former self. Libby smiled. Dr. Stillman turned in her direction and saluted.

Thus began a routine for the next three days. Dr. Stillman checked on Vance morning and evening, but there was still no change. He had little appetite, but made a valiant effort so the nurses wouldn't scold him.

On the ninth day, he moved around the room as he had before the operation. With the use of a cane, he tapped his way into the corridor and got himself a drink from the refrigerator behind the nursing station. He had a confident facade, but Libby could sense his discontent, his fear. Around nine that evening, Dr. Stillman came in to see him. Vance sprawled in a chair in front of the television set, with his head resting against the cushions. He'd removed his glasses, and they dangled from his hand. From the angle where Libby sat, he looked like any normal sighted person who'd fallen asleep out of sheer boredom.

Dr. Stillman shook him gently. "Vance? Come up on the bed. I want to examine you."

Slowly, Vance rose to his feet and went over to the bed, levering himself onto the mattress. He submitted to the doctor's ministrations without comment.

The doctor seemed to be taking an inordinately long time. "You're healing perfectly, Vance. Your general health is excellent. Any change?"

"No."

"I'm not surprised. Those nerves don't want to function again. They're feisty little creatures."

"John!" Vance gripped the other man's forearm. "Don't humor me. I can see through it."

"Then you can see more than I can. You're still within the normal time frame of recovery. After ten days postop, then I'll start to humor you. All right?"

Libby heard the sharp intake of breath. "I'm sorry." His hand dropped away.

"Don't be. You're handling all this much better than many people in this situation. I'll see you in the morning. Before you go to sleep, I'm sending in a couple of nurses to give you a rubdown. It will help you to relax."

Libby took a chance and slipped out into the hall with the doctor. "Will you let me be one of the nurses? Just this once? I'll leave everything to Mrs. Grady."

"I don't see why not."

A few minutes later, she and the matron entered Vance's room carrying towels and lotion. "All right, Mr. Anson. Time for your rubdown. Take off the glasses and turn over."

He expelled a sigh and put the glasses on the side table. Then, with a grimace, he removed his pajama top and stretched out full-length on top of the sheet. The broad, whipcord strength of his bronzed back mesmerized Libby. Cautiously, she squeezed on some lotion, then started to massage one side of his back and his right arm, while Mrs. Grady took care of the other.

"That feels heavenly, Mrs. Grady."

"It's supposed to. Just try and fall asleep." She chattered and soothed like a loving mother as she kneaded his muscles with a practiced touch. Libby moved her hands to the back of his neck and rubbed the taut cords till they started to soften. The urge to press her cheek to his back, to hold him in her arms proved too much for her. She turned away. It hadn't been a good idea to touch him, after all.

"Don't stop now," he groaned. "I'll pay you to keep going. A day's salary for a half hour more."

Mrs. Grady's full laugh rang through the air. It even brought a faint smile to Libby's lips. "Go on with you, Mr. Anson. I've other patients to see. Come along, Sister." She darted a look at Libby, then left the room.

From her position in the corner chair, Libby watched Vance as he slipped on his pajama top and settled beneath the covers for the night. She heard him sigh from time to time, but the back rub must have done some good because he didn't seem restless. Usually she went to the hotel when he settled down to sleep, but tonight she lingered. Vance might get his sight back at any moment now.

Much as she wanted to be with him when the time came, she decided to wait for news at the hotel. Charles and Dr. Stillman would keep her informed of any changes. She couldn't go on being in the same room with him when everything inside her cried out to hold him, love him. She didn't want to be responsible for a setback if he discovered her presence. And though she hated to entertain the thought that his sight might never return, she felt he deserved his privacy. Once he left the hospital, she'd decide how best to make herself part of his life again. Deep in thought, she didn't notice him get out of bed until she saw him reach for his cane. When did he wake up?

He came back to the room a minute later with a can of Coke, Mrs. Grady following in hot pursuit. "Now, Mr. Anson. How do you expect to get a decent sleep if you drink caffeine in the middle of the night? Shame on you."

"I won't tell if you won't." He grinned in the direction of the short woman, who clucked her tongue in exaggerated reproach.

He stood not five feet away from Libby, strong and fit. His lean, hard good looks seemed, oddly enough, to be emphasized by his sleeping apparel; his pallor only added to his attractiveness. He looked the same, and yet he looked different. Sometimes when Vance gazed in Libby's direction, she couldn't believe he couldn't see her. She had the same impression now, as he laughed and joked with Mrs. Grady. No one would ever guess he'd lost his sight. Libby stared. Vance seemed to be handling the waiting period well. The longer he went without showing signs of restoration, the less morose he became. While she, in turn, felt her spirits plummet. Maybe Vance had waited too long. Maybe she wanted his sight to come back too much. But not for her own sake.

Mrs. Grady watched him like a hawk. After the last swallow, she ordered him back to bed, and warned him of the consequences if he got up again. His mocking laughter followed her out of the room, a happy sound. A sound Libby hadn't heard for an eternity.

She sat in absolute quiet. A half hour passed. She could hear the slow, even sounds of his breathing. He'd fallen asleep.

Gathering her shoes in one hand, she got up and tiptoed over to the bed for one last look. He lay on his side, the pillow folded in half beneath his dark head. She leaned forward to study his face, marveling anew at the firm mold of mouth, now relaxed in sleep. No strain lines. He seemed at peace. More than anything in the world, she wanted to reach out and finger the stray brown curl of hair lying against his forehead. A feeling of intense love and tenderness caused her eyes to moisten. He'd been so brave, so strong. "Please, God." She mouthed the words before turning to leave.

"Libby?"

She gasped and turned disbelieving eyes toward him. He sat up in the hospital bed and put his feet to the floor. An orange glow from the night-light on the wall nearby threw his distinctive features into stark relief.

"Did you really think I wouldn't know the touch of your hands? The scent of your skin? When a blind man makes love, Libby, his other senses come wonderfully alive—did you know that? The night I made you mine, the night I worshiped you with my body, the exquisite touch of you made an indelible impression on my mind. I want to know your touch again. Come over here, Libby."

His words confounded her. If he meant to love her and then reject her again, she couldn't take it. Fear clutched at her heart.

"Vance, I swear I didn't intend for you to know that I'd been here." Hot tears trickled out of her eyes. "Forgive me. I'd never hurt you on purpose. I wanted to be close to you. Everyone else has been able to wait on you but me. I couldn't bear it any longer. I'm sorry." She swallowed hard. "I'll go."

"Don't be frightened of me, sweetheart." His tender entreaty disarmed her. His hands fell between his legs in an attitude of abject defeat. "Have I done so much damage that my own wife is terrified of me? Would it help if I told you life wouldn't be worth living without you? Blind or not? That the thought of facing one more second without holding you in my arms is ten thousand times worse than the loss of my sight?"

Libby couldn't breathe. It seemed she'd been waiting all her life to hear those words. A low moan escaped her throat.

"I love you, Libby. I need you more than life itself. If you'll give me another chance, I want to be a real husband to you. Our love exists in and of itself. You've proved that to me. Neither time nor circumstances have any bearing on what we feel for each other.... What we've always felt."

He took a shuddering breath. "You have every right to despise me for the way I've treated you, but please don't turn away from me." His voice shook with raw need.

Libby covered the short distance between them, insinuating herself between his legs to clasp his head to her breast.

"I love you so much," she whispered into his dark brown hair. "Oh, Vance...if your sight doesn't come back, please, please, don't let it matter. I need you. I'd do anything for you. I adore you."

His arms closed around her slender body and he clung to her for endless moments. "Nothing matters anymore except that you love me, Libby. Forgive me for throwing our marriage vows in your face. Thank God you held on."

Libby held him tighter, unable to speak. She wondered if a person could die from too much happiness exploding inside.

"When the anesthetic wore off, all I wanted was you." His hand tightened in her hair. "Then I remembered that you were on a plane back to London. I swear that was worse than finding out I was blind. The thought of another man winning your love, having the right to make love to you, drove me out of my mind. I prayed you back here, Libby."

She nuzzled his throat. "But I never left."

His body shook. "You put on a convincing performance, Mrs. Anson. When you told me you'd give me a divorce, it felt like I'd just been sentenced to the outer darkness."

"I lied. I had to. I couldn't think of anything else to do for the time being. But you have my solemn promise that I'll never knowingly lie to you again."

He pressed hot kisses against her tender neck. "Don't ever leave me. That's all I ask. When I felt your hands a while ago, I thought I was dreaming. After the way I've behaved, I was afraid to believe that my prayers had been answered."

Libby eased onto his lap, covering his face with gentle kisses, still unable to believe any of this was really happening. If it was a dream, she never wanted to wake up. "I couldn't leave you, Vance. Life has no meaning without you," she confessed, twisting her fingers into his dark curls. "I can't pretend to know what it's like to be blind, but I can honestly tell you that it couldn't be any worse than imagining a life without you. Talk about your outer darkness!" Her lower lip trembled. "That first day in your hospital room, when you told me to go back home—that I wasn't wanted—I felt as if I'd been sentenced to the worst kind of misery...because you wouldn't be there."

"Forgive me for putting you through this?" he whispered against her mouth.

"There's nothing to forgive. I love you," she whispered back.

Then his hungry mouth covered hers with an aching tenderness that quickly changed to something else as they marveled at the depth of their love.

In a swift sure movement, Vance lifted her in his arms and put her on the bed, sliding onto the mattress beside her. "As soon as Dr. Stillman releases me from the hospital, we'll leave on a honeymoon. I don't want to share you with anyone for months and months. It's going to take me that long to believe this is really happening." His hands moved over her. "But you are real, aren't you, my love, and so beautiful. So beautiful it hurts."

The little moaning sounds were her own as Libby could no longer contain her joy, but she reminded herself that they were in a hospital room. Right now she was in danger of forgetting everything. "Vance— anyone could walk in on us," she murmured huskily against his chin, where she felt the beginnings of a beard.

"I'm paying for this room while I'm here. If I want to hold my wife, that's no one's concern, but mine," he said in a tone that recalled the Vance she'd known before the accident—confident and self-assured. "Just wait till I get you home, Mrs. Anson."

"I love it when you call me that," she admitted, nestling closer, if that was even possible.

"Libby, as soon as Martin and the others are formally charged, we'll go away—anyplace you choose."

"I'd just as soon hibernate at the farm if you want to know the truth."

"The farm?" He raised up on one elbow, his expression one of astonishment and wonder.

"It's the most beautiful place in the world to me. Please, please don't sell it. I couldn't bear it."

An exultant laugh came rumbling out of him. "Oh, Libby, Libby." He crushed her in his arms. "I don't deserve you."

"Why do you say that?" she whispered against his neck.

"You've just erased my greatest worry. From the very beginning, I've wondered if I was doing the right thing by you."

"Vance?" She lifted her head so she could look at him. "What do you mean?"

He lowered his mouth to hers for a long moment. "I don't think you have any conception of how I felt when I first met you. If we weren't living in civilized society, I would have abducted you from my father's drawing room and taken you back to Kenya with me that very night. As it was, you were still in school and I had no idea if you could stand being uprooted from the life you were used to. That's why I waited almost three years to ask you to marry me. But on the last visit, I couldn't take any more. Still, I was terrified you mightn't like the isolation of the highlands." He kissed her hard. "On that first day at the farm, you sounded so happy, but I didn't dare believe it. I thought you were pretending for *my* benefit. Let me hold you, Libby," he said urgently. "Let me love you for the rest of our lives."

LAVENDER RAYS OF DAWN filtered through the hospital room window and fell across the bed hours later. Libby felt the warmth of the early-morning light on her face and stirred, but was held fast in her husband's arms.

She opened her eyes to discover that Vance was awake. His dark, velvety brown eyes played over her features, almost caressing the delicate lines of her facial structure. There was a difference in the way he looked at her—a knowledge that had been missing since the accident. Her breath caught in her throat.

"Vance?"

"Don't move," he whispered. "Lie still. Let me look at you, Libby. If my eyes don't deceive me, you're wearing a pale blue skirt and blouse with navy and white trim on the hem and collar. Am I dreaming?" Anxiety warred with disbelief in his voice.

Libby's eyes blurred with tears as she stared at her husband. "It's no dream. Your sight—it's come back!" She lifted a hand to his face, tracing his dark brow with a gentle finger. "W-when did it happen?" She swallowed hard, hoping—praying—they weren't both part of the same dream.

"I'm not sure," he muttered, raising himself up to a sitting position. "I woke up a while ago and saw everything in a shadow. I closed my eyes, wondering what it could mean. The next time I opened them, I saw your face as clear as a bell. The only problem is, your image has been impressed on my mind and my heart for so long, I thought—I assumed—Libby?" he cried out. "I can really see you!" His eyes glistened with tears. "My beautiful, adorable wife."

His keen glance darted everywhere, taking in the wanton disarray of her glistening black hair. "Did you know that when you're emotional, your eyes glow with a purple fire? And your lower lip trembles?" He leaned over and kissed it quiet, running firm hands over her shoulders and down her arms, drawing her hands to his chest. "Your faith did it, Libby." The humility in his voice was something she'd remember all her life.

A radiant smile broke on her face. "Dr. Stillman said someone arranged that accident while we were out riding."

He lifted her hands and kissed the palms with a gentleness that touched her heart. "What if you'd given up on me? What if you'd gone back to London that first day?" He gathered her in his arms once more. "Don't ever leave me. Don't ever stop loving me."

"Good morning, Mr. Anson," Mrs. Grady's voice resounded as she swept into the room. "It's a lovely morning." She stopped short. "Mr. Anson!"

Libby tore her lips from Vance's and slid off the bed, attempting to straighten her rumpled skirt and blouse. Vance started to chuckle, his white smile dazzling. "It is indeed a lovely, glorious morning, Mrs. Grady. I had no idea your eyes were such a bonny blue."

"So! Your sight's come back, has it?" Her eyes twinkled. "Well, now. Under the circumstances, I won't report what I just saw. But remember that Dr. Stillman will be on his rounds in a few minutes. We wouldn't want to give the poor man heart failure now, would we? Not after what he's done for you."

"No, Mrs. Grady." He folded his arms and grinned at Libby. "I'm taking my bride out of here this morning, so let me say goodbye and thank you. I couldn't have had more loving care if you'd been my own mother.''

"Ah, go on with you, Mr. Anson.'' She beamed like a young girl. "Your kind can charm the birds from the trees. You be good to this lovely bride of yours. She's stood guard over you, watching you, praying for you. She hasn't left your side for a second, and she put up with you when nobody else knew what to do with you. Where I come from, we say she has the gift of the good fairy."

"What gift is that, Mrs. Grady?" he asked thickly.

"A constant heart, Mr. Anson. Something rare, indeed."

Libby grasped the hand he extended toward her as Mrs. Grady left the room. The sun had come up over the horizon. She went back into his arms—where she belonged.

Vance stared down at her with an intensity that held her spellbound. "You, Libby, and only you, brought a blind man out of the darkest abyss into the light," he said with tears in his voice. "I want to give you the world in return."

Her luminous eyes blazed a vibrant purple. "You already did that when you asked me to marry you. But I want to forget the world for a while and just be alone with you. I've been thinking about the possibility of our baby growing inside me, Vance. And I want that to happen soon—if it hasn't already." She gently pushed him back against the mattress and lowered her mouth to his in a deep, lingering kiss.

The sound of voices outside the door caused Libby to lift her head, but Vance trapped her flushed face in his hands. "I hoped you'd say that, Mrs. Anson. Because I have no intention of letting you out of my arms—or my sight—for a long time to come."

Harlequin American Romance

**Romances that go one step farther...
American Romance**

Realistic stories involving people you can relate to and care about.

Compelling relationships between the mature men and women of today's world.

Romances that capture the core of genuine emotions between a man and a woman.

Join us each month for four new titles wherever paperback books are sold.
Enter the world of American Romance.

Harlequin Temptation dares to be different!

Once in a while, we Temptation editors spot a romance that's truly innovative. To make sure *you* don't miss any one of these outstanding selections, we'll mark them for you.

EDITOR'S CHOICE

When the "Editors' Choice" fold-back appears on a Temptation cover, you'll know we've found that extra-special page-turner!

THE

Temptation

EDITORS

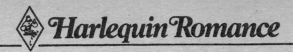
Harlequin Romance

Coming Next Month

2959 PAINTED LADY Diana Hamilton
Ziggy, reunited with her grandfather in England, revises her opinion of him and the family feud that separated them. But she won't change her opinion of Rafe d'Anjou. She's sure his interest in bringing her and her grandfather together, and in herself, is entirely selfish.

2960 ONLY MY DREAMS Rowan Kirby
A true romantic and dreamer, Erinna is furious when her staid Midlands tutor, Dr. John Bryce, cautions her against taking life at face value. What does he know, she fumes, a man seemingly impervious to any real emotion himself!

2961 ALWAYS A BRIDESMAID Patricia Knoll
Shelby Featherstone wants store space in A. J. Court's exclusive San Diego mall—not a ring on her finger. And especially not the heartache of having to plan his real fiancée's wedding!

2962 STORM CLOUDS GATHERING Edwina Shore
Everyone is keen to tell Jenna that Drew Merrick is back on the Australian island where they both grew up—but nobody can tell her why. Certainly it's the last thing Jenna needs just when she's made up her mind to marry Adam.

2963 YESTERDAY'S ENEMY Lee Stafford
Ten years ago Steve Rodriguez had deprived Nicole's stepfather of his livelihood, so it's ironic when her job lands her back at the scene of the crime. Will Steve recognize her as "young Nicky"? And if he does, how should she react?

2964 WITHOUT LOVE Jessica Steele
Kassia lost her job because of Lyon Mulholland, who even blocked her subsequent efforts to get another one. So her feelings for him bordered on hatred. Yet when he makes handsome amends, she finds her troubles are only just starting....

Available in February wherever paperback books are sold, or through Harlequin Reader Service:

In the U.S.
901 Fuhrmann Blvd.
P.O. Box 1397
Buffalo, N.Y. 14240-1397

In Canada
P.O. Box 603
Fort Erie, Ontario
L2A 5X3

Keepsake

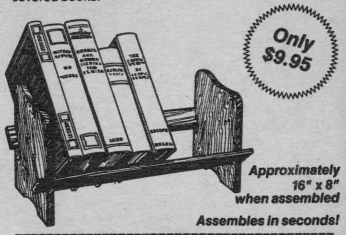